Thespian Playworks 2013

The Actuality of Henrik
by Jacob Sellers

The Christian Soothsayer
by Aaron Robertson

The Crib
by Steve Rathje

Houdini Will Die
by Sage Voorhees

A SAMUEL FRENCH ACTING EDITION

SAMUEL FRENCH

FOUNDED 1830

SAMUELFRENCH.COM
SAMUELFRENCH-LONDON.CO.UK

ISBN 978-0-573-70290-7

www.SamuelFrench.com
www.SamuelFrench-London.co.uk

FOR PRODUCTION ENQUIRIES

UNITED STATES AND CANADA
Info@SamuelFrench.com
1-866-598-8449

UNITED KINGDOM AND EUROPE
Plays@SamuelFrench-London.co.uk
020-7255-4302

Each title is subject to availability from Samuel French, depending upon country of performance. Please be aware that *THESPIAN PLAYWORKS 2013* may not be licensed by Samuel French in your territory. Professional and amateur producers should contact the nearest Samuel French office or licensing partner to verify availability.

MUSIC USE NOTE

IMPORTANT BILLING AND CREDIT REQUIREMENTS

CONTENTS

The Actuality of Henrik

by Jacob Sellers

THE ACTUALITY OF HENRIK was presented in a staged reading as part of the Thespian Playworks program at the 2013 Thespian Festival on June 29, 2013. The reading was directed by Dominic Orlando, with dramaturgy by Lindsay Price and stage management by Brie Greer. The cast was as follows:

GEORGE... David Branson
PAULYNA .... Carly Kerr
RHYSE..Tucker Breder
PERDITA...................................Samantha A. Murphy
ONE... Sharmaine Velasco
TWO.................................. McKenzie Graham-Howard
THREE .... Dylan Arredondo

ABOUT THE PLAYWRIGHT

Jacob Sellers is a native of Fort Branch, Indiana—or maybe Indiana, Fort Branch. Fort Indiana, Branch? Who knows. He originally wrote *The Actuality* in his junior year at Gibson Southern High School, where a production was put on starring Kirstin Connor, Owen Gick, Dominik Richardville, and Kaitlyn Roth. Or maybe it wasn't. As Jacob prepares to begin his schooling as a theatre generalist at the University of Evansville, he'd like to thank all those at Thespian Playworks, his brilliant original cast, and every other living and non-living person. (Except for the help; the help aren't persons.)

CHARACTERS

GEORGE – The straight man. Not too angry.
PAULYNA – Pronounced "Paul-eye-na." She appears to control the room and know nearly everything.
RHYSE – Pronounced like "rise." Her puppet.
PERDITA – Difficult.
ONE – Quiet.
TWO – The leader.
THREE – Loud.
CHILDREN – Starving.

NOTES

CASTING – I believe each character could be any race, age, or possibly gender. I've seen the children played by One, Two, and Three, and I've seen them played by actual children. I think both work well. I also think it could be funny to have them played by dolls. Maybe that's too straightforward.

DELIVERY – Pay attention to the presence of commas or lack thereof.

COSTUMES – I'm not too particular on this, though I think George would be in rather realistic, neutral clothing. I'd imagine the others could vary.

DESIGN – The show could be in a living room or it could not be.

PROPS

Three dictionaries, laminator, word search, pen, birth certificate, knife, bandage, two sheets of plastic, pillow (fake baby), juice box, flask, party hats, talking stick, pills, two bowls, two spoons, phone, bottle of water, rag, rice, rose petals, electric candles, gavel, masks, two guns, small lamp (fake baby).

(ONE, TWO, and THREE walk onstage and stand in numerical order.)

TWO. A few announcements before the show begins.

ONE. All flash photography must be turned on during the performance.

THREE. Texting, talking, eating, drinking, and smoking are strictly prohibited outside the theater.

TWO. In case of a fire, the emergency exits are located nowhere. *(Pause.)* The following events are

ALL THREE. Based on a true story.

TWO. Everything you see before you is

ONE. 100%.

THREE. Beyond a doubt.

TWO. Satisfaction guaranteed.

ALL THREE. True.

TWO. In the name of the father.

ONE. And of the son.

THREE. And of the holy spirit...

ALL THREE. Shalom.

> *(ALL THREE spread out and sit down. We could be in a living room, but then again not. The stage is covered with furniture—couches, chairs, coffee tables, the like—all centered around a bed in which GEORGE is sleeping.)*
>
> *(PAULYNA and RHYSE sit together, watching GEORGE. PAULYNA is extremely pregnant.)*
>
> *(PERDITA laminates paper.)*
>
> *(A child does a word search at a desk.)*

PAULYNA. I do hope he wakes up soon.

RHYSE. I'm sure he will.

PAULYNA. You don't think he's dead, do you?

RHYSE. I don't. But I can't know. There's no way to. *(stands to feel* **GEORGE**'*s pulse)* His heart is beating, but the heart tells lies. For all we know, he hasn't even lived yet, much less experienced death.

PAULYNA. How philosophical of you, honey.

*(***GEORGE*** wakes up. He looks around for some time before speaking.)*

GEORGE. Where am I?

*(***PAULYNA*** laughs.)*

PAULYNA. Very funny, Doctor. Where did you learn to be so funny?

RHYSE. He was a comedian in his youth, remember?

PAULYNA. Yes, I do. I have a photographic memory.

GEORGE. No, I wasn't. I was never a comedian.

PAULYNA. Of course not; doctors aren't funny.

RHYSE. Especially not you.

GEORGE. I'm not a doctor.

*(***PAULYNA*** laughs.)*

PAULYNA. He is a comedian.

GEORGE. What's going on?

PAULYNA. You're waking up from a nap, Doctor. Or death. Or the womb. No one knows the secrets of the heart.

GEORGE. How did I get here?

PAULYNA. We laid you here when you asked for the bed.

GEORGE. Me?

PAULYNA. Yes. I was in the middle of labor and you had grown tired of delivering the baby, so we paused while you napped.

GEORGE. Where's the baby now?

PAULYNA. In my uterus. Or large intestine. My aim isn't what it used to be.

GEORGE. What?!

PAULYNA. When you asked for the bed, I pushed the baby back up to keep it warm until you were ready.

(**GEORGE** *is speechless.*)

I do hope you're ready soon though. It's starting to hit.

GEORGE. I have no idea how to deliver a child.

PAULYNA. You've delivered all of our others; I don't know why you would forget now. Unless you lose your earthly skills in the afterlife.

GEORGE. How many children have you had?

PAULYNA. How many would you say, Rhyse?

RHYSE. Oh, how could we know? It all runs together after the first or second.

GEORGE. You don't know how many children you've had?!

RHYSE. It's at least a handful.

PAULYNA. Oh! Two handfuls! Look at that.

(*A child crawls out from under* **PAULYNA**'s *dress.*)

Wasn't that easy!

RHYSE. I felt no pain at all.

PAULYNA. You really are a great doctor, Henrik.

GEORGE. My name's not Henrik.

PAULYNA. And a great comedian.

GEORGE. My name is George.

PAULYNA. We need to name the child, Rhyse!

(**THREE** *walks up to* **PAULYNA** *and* **RHYSE.**)

THREE. I have the birth certificate, ma'am. You can write the name here.

PAULYNA. I haven't a clue how to write.

RHYSE. Much less whistle for that matter.

THREE. I'll write it for you. First name?

PAULYNA. Aibra. After the Doctor.

GEORGE. I am not a doctor.

THREE. Middle name?

GEORGE. And my name isn't Aibra.

PAULYNA. Hamlincoln.

THREE. Beautiful.

PAULYNA. We love the Bible.

RHYSE. And slavery.

GEORGE. What is going on here!?

PAULYNA. *(to* **GEORGE***)* We're naming the child. *(to* **PERDITA***)* Oh, Perdita!

(**PERDITA** *looks up from her work.*)

Please get the child's name from the man here so you can make a nametag.

GEORGE. For your child?

PAULYNA. No, for you, Henrik.

(**GEORGE** *is confused.*)

Of course for the child. Who else?

GEORGE. Is he going somewhere?

PAULYNA. You think we would let it out of the house? It doesn't even have the afterbirth out of its ears. The nametag is to remember its name.

GEORGE. Your own child's name?!

PAULYNA. Mahatmagan isn't an easy name to remember.

GEORGE. His name is Aibra!

PAULYNA. That is why we have the nametags.

GEORGE. This is terrible.

PAULYNA. It's brilliant. Perdita came up with it herself. Look.

(**PAULYNA** *calls to the child doing a word search.*)

You there! At the desk! Look up at us.

(The child looks up.)

Ah, yes. Martinloo. Our first or second child.

RHYSE. First.

PAULYNA. Your first.

RHYSE. Your second.

(GEORGE can't keep up.)

PAULYNA. The first child was Perdita and I's.

RHYSE. But then Perdita was hired to work here.

PAULYNA. And it's not right to sleep with the help.

RHYSE. So we married.

PAULYNA. Martinloo! Give your father a kiss.

(The child stands, crosses to RHYSE and gives him a kiss.)

(pointing to PERDITA) And now your mother.

GEORGE. That's the wrong child.

PAULYNA. Oh, you're right. Come back, Therking. Don't kiss the help.

GEORGE. You said his name was Martinloo.

PAULYNA. We often call our children by their middle names. Return to your Sudoku, Therking.

GEORGE. He doesn't even have a nametag.

PAULYNA. Does he not? Hm. Doesn't matter. I make them up either way.

(THREE walks up to PAULYNA.)

THREE. Your guests are here.

PAULYNA. What did he say, Rhyse? My sight is fading.

RHYSE. He said the cat died.

PAULYNA. Lie to me.

RHYSE. The cat had kittens.

PAULYNA. Oh! Let's name them!

(PAULYNA, RHYSE, and THREE exit.)

(GEORGE looks around the room. He sees PERDITA laminating papers.)

PERDITA. Yes?

GEORGE. What is going on here?

(PERDITA doesn't respond.)

Hello?

PERDITA. Piss off.

> (**TWO**, *still reading, laughs.* **GEORGE** *tries to figure out if he's hurt or mad.*)

> (**PERDITA** *looks up and smiles.*)

I'm joking.

ONE. Joke. A noun. A statement, rhyme, or saying told to produce laughter. A verb. Meaning to tell a joke, to kid, to tease, or other such Tomfoolery.

GEORGE. What is that?

PERDITA. A definition.

GEORGE. I know that.

PERDITA. To help you understand words.

GEORGE. I know what "joke" means.

PERDITA. Good job.

GEORGE. Ugh.

ONE. Ugh. An exasperation. Showing frustration, annoyan –

GEORGE. I don't need definitions!

> (**PERDITA** *looks at* **GEORGE** *for a moment. Smiles.*)

PERDITA. Come here.

GEORGE. Why?

PERDITA. Do you want help?

GEORGE. With what?

PERDITA. That paper cut.

GEORGE. I don't have a paper cut.

PERDITA. Are you sure?

GEORGE. Huh?

ONE. Sure. A noun. To be full –

GEORGE. I'm sure!

PERDITA. Come here. Let me check.

> (**GEORGE** *stands and walks to* **PERDITA**, *holds out his hand.*)

GEORGE. See. No cut.

(**PERDITA** *inspects closer.*)

PERDITA. Hm…

GEORGE. What?

(**PERDITA** *pulls out a knife and makes a long cut on the palm of* **GEORGE***'s hand.*)

PERDITA. It is a nasty one.

GEORGE. What?!

(**PERDITA** *smiles at* **GEORGE.***)*

PERDITA. Let me clean that up.

(**PERDITA** *slaps a bandage on the cut and puts* **GEORGE***'s hand between two sheets of plastic. She begins to feed the plastic and sandwiched hand into the laminator.*)

GEORGE. WHAT are you doing?

PERDITA. Laminating.

GEORGE. My hand?!

(**GEORGE** *pulls his hand away.* **PAULYNA, RHYSE, THREE,** *and several children walk onstage. We can only assume* **PAULYNA** *is pregnant, though her "baby" seems to be just a pillow shoved up her dress.*)

PAULYNA. This is the brown room. When was it built, Rhyse?

RHYSE. Built is an abstract term.

PAULYNA. It is. I hate Pollack. (*Changing the subject, gesturing to* **PERDITA.***)* Normally we don't allow the help in here, but since it's the holiday – oh, did you get lost, boy?

GEORGE. Boy?

PAULYNA. Just go ahead and rejoin the group. You didn't miss much… Perdita, we found these children in the barn outside. The cat had humans.

PERDITA. Are they yours?

PAULYNA. One can only hope.

GEORGE. I'm not your child.

PAULYNA. Don't contradict your father. I distinctly remember you being born.

RHYSE. I don't. But then again I don't remember my own mother being born.

PAULYNA. That reminds me, Perdita! Rhyse and I are expecting.

GEORGE. What?!

PAULYNA. We'll need you to prepare for delivery. *(To the group.)* Perdita delivers all of our children.

GEORGE. Huh?

PAULYNA. Don't you remember?

GEORGE. What about the doctor?

PAULYNA. We don't believe in ghosts.

RHYSE. We're democrats.

GEORGE. Four minutes ago you said I needed to deliver your child.

PAULYNA. No.

GEORGE.... Yes.

> *(PAULYNA looks at GEORGE with pity, as though witnessing a starving African orphan.)*

PAULYNA. I drank while I had you, didn't I?

GEORGE.....huh?

PAULYNA. I drank during one of the pregnancies. Can't remember which one.

PERDITA. It's this one.

> *(PERDITA points to PAULYNA's stomach. PAULYNA looks down.)*

PAULYNA. Oh! You're right.

> *(PAULYNA pulls a juice box out of her bra.)*

GEORGE. I thought you meant alcohol.

> *(PAULYNA pulls a flask out of her sleeve.)*

PAULYNA. That too.

GEORGE. But you're having a baby!

PAULYNA. Oh, don't worry. Rhyse never drinks while we're pregnant.

GEORGE. I have to sit down.

PAULYNA. You can't sit down now. The party's nearly started.

GEORGE. Party?

(The children all take out party hats and put them on their heads. **RHYSE** *puts two on like a bra à la Madonna.* **PAULYNA** *puts hers on her stomach à la a unicorn with a horn on its stomach.)*

(To **PERDITA**.*)* You're not wearing one?

PERDITA. I don't wear hats.

PAULYNA. This is a church, Henrik. Honestly.

GEORGE. I thought this was a party.

PAULYNA. For me?!

*(***PAULYNA** *looks around in shock.)*

(To **GEORGE**.*)* You threw a surprise party for me?!

GEORGE. No.

RHYSE. I don't know when your birthday is.

PERDITA. It was me.

PAULYNA. How thoughtful of you, Perdita. We should feed you this month.

PERDITA. It's why I'm living.

PAULYNA. Everyone take a seat. I ordered mashed potatoes.

(Everyone sits cross-legged in a circle on the floor.)

GEORGE. You ordered? I thought this was a surprise.

PAULYNA. Yes, for Nelsonman. *(Gestures to one of the sitting children.)*

GEORGE. It's not your birthday?

PAULYNA. Every day is my birthday. Tell us, Dela. What is your fondest memory?

(The child opens its mouth.)

Quiet, only Perdita can talk. She has the stick.

(**PERDITA** *grabs a stick off of a couch next to her.*)

Your fondest memory, Perdita.

PERDITA. My fondest memory is when I was six and I was happy.

PAULYNA. All of my memories are fond.

RHYSE. None of mine are.

PAULYNA. We should get divorced.

RHYSE. I signed the papers.

PAULYNA. Enough about us. This party is for Nelsonman. We're going to sing. Stand, Dela.

(*The child stands.*)

Sing, Henrik.

GEORGE. I can't sing.

PAULYNA. Sing.

GEORGE. I can't –

PAULYNA. SING!

GEORGE. (*singing*) Happy Birthday to y–

PAULYNA. Wrong.

GEORGE. What?

PAULYNA. That's the wrong song.

GEORGE. It's the birthday song.

PAULYNA. Why would you assume it's someone's birthday?

GEORGE. The birthday hat. That you have on your stomach.

PAULYNA. Was that a fat joke?!

GEORGE. No!

RHYSE. Calm down, honey.

PAULYNA. Really, Henrik. Do you have to bring race into this?

GEORGE. I wasn't bringing anything –

PAULYNA. Just sing the song.

GEORGE. Ha–

PAULYNA. NOT THAT SONG!

GEORGE. WHAT DO YOU WANT ME TO SING!?

PAULYNA. LONDON BRIDGE!

GEORGE. *(singing)*
LONDON BRIDGE IS –

PAULYNA. LOUDER!

GEORGE.
LONDON BRIDGE IS FALLING DOWN,
FALLING DOWN, FALLING DOW –

PAULYNA. BOO! BOO! BOOOOO! YOU SUCK! YOU-SUCK-YOU-SUCK-YOU-SUCK-YOU-I'm-so-sorry-Henrik-it's-the-hormones…

(PAULYNA collapses.)

I'm so sorry. It's the baby. I didn't mean to snap like that. Normally it's much more dramatic..

GEORGE. It's…it's fine.

(RHYSE tries to calm PAULYNA.)

PAULYNA. I've ruined everything. And on your birthday…

GEORGE. It's not my birthday.

(PAULYNA is immediately better.)

PAULYNA. Oh then never mind. What time is it, Rhyse?

RHYSE. Time is an illusion.

PAULYNA. Bring out our dinner, Perdita.

(PERDITA brings over two bowls, pours pills in them, and then adds water.)

You're welcome.

PERDITA. Thank you.

PAULYNA. Now exit and pursue that bear.

PERDITA. Yes, Your Grace.

(PERDITA exits to pursue the bear.)

PAULYNA. I must say, Rhyse. This has to be the best anniversary party we've had in years.

RHYSE. I couldn't agree whore.

(GEORGE walks over to the bed at sits down. A squeal comes from beneath the covers. GEORGE jumps up. A small child pops up from under the covers.)

PAULYNA. Watch what you're doing! You can't just sit down on a person's bed.

GEORGE. That's my bed.

PAULYNA. WHY IS THERE A CHILD IN YOUR BED?!

GEORGE. I had no idea!

PAULYNA. Rhyse, call the cops.

GEORGE. I'm not a pedophile!

PAULYNA. Oh shush, you love feet. I'm having my baby! Please call them, Rhyse. Hurry.

(RHYSE dials the police.)

RHYSE. Hello? Police? Yes, my wife is having a ball.

PAULYNA. No, Rhyse!

RHYSE. Did I misspeak?

PAULYNA. A blast! I'm having a blast!

RHYSE. Sorry! *(To the cops.)* She's having a blast! *(Pause.)* Yes. *(Pause.)* Yes. *(Pause.)* I know, I know. *(Pause. Laughs.)* You're welcome. *(Pause.)* Goodbye. *(Hangs up.)* They didn't answer!

PAULYNA. Thank goodness!

(PAULYNA and RHYSE walk over to GEORGE's bed.)

Come on, children. You won't want to miss this.

(PAULYNA and RHYSE and the children get down on the floor and crawl under the bed to deliver the baby. PERDITA enters and crawls under the bed with a bottle of water and a rag and rice.)

(From under the bed.) Oh thank God you're back, Perdita. No one missed you.

GEORGE. *(Not following the others, standing.)* What is happening!?

PERDITA. *(From under the bed.)* Okay, ready?

RHYSE. *(From under the bed.)* Yes.

PERDITA. *(From under the bed.)* One. Two. THREE!

PAULYNA. *(From under the bed.)* Good job, Perdita! That's the highest number you've ever gotten to!

PERDITA. *(From under the bed.)* Thank you, master. I've been practicing.

PAULYNA. *(From under the bed.)* Shut up, Perdita. Don't speak unless spoken to.

*(**THREE** walks up to the bed with a birth certificate.)*

THREE. We need a name for the child, ma'am.

PAULYNA. *(From under the bed.)* What child? *(Pause.)* Oh. There it is. I thought my stomach seemed lighter.

RHYSE. *(From under the bed.)* All of that exercise has paid off.

PAULYNA. *(From under the bed.)* Exercise is a myth.

THREE. The name?

PAULYNA. *(From under the bed.)* Oh, yes… Osamabin.

THREE. Adorable.

GEORGE. What?!

PAULYNA. *(From under the bed.)* After Rhyse's mother.

RHYSE. *(From under the bed.)* Or brother.

PAULYNA. *(From under the bed.)* Only the gods know.

GEORGE. I have to get out of here.

*(**TWO** stands.)*

TWO. *(To the audience.)* We will now pause for a brief 15-second intermission. *(To the actors.)* Actors, fifteen.

ALL BUT GEORGE. Thank you, fifteen.

*(The house lights come up. Everyone on stage exits. **GEORGE** is confused at first, but then follows suit.)*

(After ten seconds, the house lights flicker.)

(After fifteen seconds, the house lights go back down and the stage lights come up.)

TWO. And we're back.

ALL BUT GEORGE. Thank you, back.

(ONE, TWO, and THREE read from the dictionary.)

TWO. Truth. Noun. The conformity with fact or reality.

ONE. The state or character of being true.

THREE. Actuality, fax the cow to me.

> *(RHYSE stands. PAULYNA is not in the room. PERDITA is tossing rose petals on the ground.)*

> *(GEORGE wakes up in his bed. He starts to say something, but then sees another way out. He watches.)*

RHYSE. What am I doing?

PERDITA. Undressing.

RHYSE. Why am I undressing?

PERDITA. You're going to lovemake.

RHYSE. Okay.

> *(RHYSE takes off his tie.)*

PERDITA. Lie down.

> *(RHYSE lies down.)*

RHYSE. Why am I going to lovemake?

PERDITA. Because you love your wife.

RHYSE. I'm not married.

PERDITA. Yes you are.

RHYSE. I forgot.

PERDITA. No you didn't.

RHYSE. No I didn't.

> *(PERDITA turns on electric candles and places them about the stage.)*

I think I love my wife.

PERDITA. You do.

RHYSE. How do you know?

PERDITA. How do you know?

RHYSE. You're right.

> *(PERDITA pauses. She looks at RHYSE lying motionlessly on the floor.)*

PERDITA. You don't.

RHYSE. I don't know?

PERDITA. You don't love your wife.

RHYSE. I don't love my wife.

PERDITA. You don't love your wife.

RHYSE. I don't love my wife.

PERDITA. I know.

RHYSE. You know.

PERDITA. Open your mouth.

> (**RHYSE** *opens his mouth.*)

> (**PERDITA** *drops rose petals into it. She places an electric candle in it as well.*)

> (**PAULYNA** *enters.*)

PAULYNA. I'm ready to lovemake because I love my husband!

RHYSE. *(With the rose petals and candle in his mouth.)* I'm ready to lovemake because I love my wife!

> (**PAULYNA** *walks over to* **RHYSE** *and looks down upon him.*)

PAULYNA. You're the stupidest person I ever met.

> (**RHYSE** *nods in agreement.*)

Let's lovemake because we love each other.

> (**RHYSE** *stands and he and* **PAULYNA** *walk over to* **GEORGE***'s bed.*)

> (**GEORGE** *had been hiding up until this time, but as* **PAULYNA** *and* **RHYSE** *climb in to the bed, he sits up.*)

GEORGE. No!

PAULYNA. Oh, Henrik! I was just climbing into bed so I could lovemake with my husband because I love him.

> (**PAULYNA** *looks at* **RHYSE**. *He doesn't do anything.*)

Your line.

RHYSE. I don't know it.

PAULYNA. It's okay. It's because you're stupid.

RHYSE. Line.

PERDITA. *(Reading from a script in her hands.)* I was just climbing into bed so I could lovemake with my husband because I love him.

RHYSE. I was just climbing into bed so I could lovemake with my husb– I don't have a husband.

PAULYNA. That's a plot hole.

RHYSE. I don't think I love *you* either.

PAULYNA. You do. You're just stupid.

RHYSE. No I don't.

> **(PAULYNA** *pounces on* **RHYSE** *and begins to strangle him.)*

PAULYNA. YES YOU DO!

RHYSE. Perdita told me I didn't!

> **(PAULYNA** *looks at* **PERDITA.***)*

PERDITA. No I didn't. He's just stupid.

> **(PAULYNA** *stops strangling him and holds him with pity.)*

PAULYNA. You do love me.

RHYSE. No I don't.

PAULYNA. You do. I'll show you.

> **(PAULYNA** *kisses* **RHYSE** *and it lasts for at least fifteen seconds. There is nothing romantic about it at all however, and they remain completely frozen throughout.)*

> *(After they're done –)*

RHYSE. I love you more than any person I've ever met.

PAULYNA. You've only met two persons.

RHYSE. I've met you and Henrik and Perdita.

PAULYNA. Perdita's not a person; she's the help.

RHYSE. The help aren't persons.

PAULYNA. Nobody are persons.

RHYSE. You're the smartest person I've ever met.

PAULYNA. I know because I'm smart.

(**GEORGE** *attempts to sneak off the bed.*)

PAULYNA. Henrik, where are you going?

GEORGE. Just – um. To get out of the bed.

PAULYNA. Well you can stay if you'd like. We can lovemake because you love me.

GEORGE. That's okay.

TWO. ORDERRRR!

(**PAULYNA** *and* **RHYSE** *stand at attention.*)

ORDER IN THE COURT!

PAULYNA. Left! Left! Left right left!

PAULYNA and **RHYSE.** Left! Left! Left right left!

(*We are now in a courtroom or at least a room in which court is being held.*)

(**PAULYNA, RHYSE,** *and* **PERDITA** *are one party and* **GEORGE** *and* **THREE** *are another.* **TWO** *is the judge.* **ONE** *is the stenographer. The children observe.*)

(**ONE** *gives everyone a mask.*)

PAULYNA. Put your mask on, Henrik. If you have a heart.

GEORGE. Why masks?

PAULYNA. Give a man a mask, and he will tell you the truth.

(**PAULYNA** *puts on her mask.*)

Man is least himself when he talks in third person.

(**TWO** *pulls out the dictionary and places* **GEORGE**'s *hand on it.*)

TWO. Do you swear to tell the truth, the whole truth, and nothing but the truth, so help your god?

GEORGE. I – yes.

(**TWO** *places* **PAULYNA**'s *hand on the dictionary.*)

TWO. Do you swear to tell the truth, the false truth, and lies accepted as the truth to help a god?

PAULYNA. Amen.

GEORGE. Wait, she can't do that.

PAULYNA. I can do all things through Christ who strengthens me.

GEORGE. You just swore to lie.

PAULYNA. The only difference between a lie and truth is that one is said more often.

(**TWO** *strikes the gavel three times and everyone sits.*)

TWO. Dearly beloved and dearly bereaved, let's get ready to rumble.

PERDITA. I call Henrik to the stand.

(**TWO** *hits the gavel.*)

TWO. The court calls Henrik to the stand.

(**GEORGE** *is confused.*)

PAULYNA. Do hurry, Henrik. We have all day.

(**GEORGE** *goes to the stand.*)

PERDITA. What were you the knight of the incident?

GEORGE. What incident?

PERDITA. Don't sass the defendant.

GEORGE. I'm not sassing, I just don't know what you're talking about!

PERDITA. No further questions.

THREE. I call her Trajesty to the stand.

(**TWO** *hits the gavel.*)

TWO. Mother of Mercy to the stand.

(**PAULYNA** *goes to the stand.* **GEORGE** *begins to go back to his seat.*)

PERDITA. YOUR HONOR! HE'S RUNNING!

GEORGE. I'm going back to my seat!

(**TWO** *hits the gavel.*)

TWO. You have the right to remain silent. (*Hits gavel, to* **THREE.**) Continue.

THREE. *(To* **PAULYNA.***)* Mother Nature, how is it that you're so perfect?

PAULYNA. Objection! Asking questions that cannot be answered.

*(***TWO** *hits the gavel.)*

TWO. Objection observed.

*(***THREE** *sits.)*

*(***PERDITA** *stands.)*

PERDITA. *(To* **GEORGE.***)* Spell "their."

GEORGE. What?

PERDITA. Spell "their."

GEORGE. What does that have to do with anything?

PERDITA. Refusal to answer questions. Guilty.

*(***TWO** *hits gavel.)*

TWO. Guilty!

THREE. Guilty!

RHYSE. SURPRISE!

PAULYNA. For me?!

GEORGE. I'll answer the question!

PERDITA. Hm?

GEORGE. Can I have a definition?

PERDITA. No.

GEORGE. I don't know which "there" you mean. I need a definition.

PERDITA. You said before you didn't need definitions. So you get none.

GEORGE. This is ridiculous.

PERDITA. No, your word is "their."

GEORGE. There. T-H-E-R-E.

*(***ONE** *dings a bell.)*

PERDITA. Sorry.

GEORGE. Which one was it?

PERDITA. You don't want to know.

PAULYNA. You're an idiot, Henrik. You can't even spell "they're."

RHYSE. He wasn't my brother.

PAULYNA. And neither mine.

PERDITA. What is the answer to this question? Is it A. All of the above, C. Some of the below, B. A and B only, or D. A?

GEORGE. How am I supposed to answer that?

PERDITA. With a letter.

GEORGE. …A.

(The bell dings.)

PERDITA. The correct answer was E. C.

*(**GEORGE** sighs.)*

What is the population of Madrid, Spain? A. One million, B. One million and one, C. One million and two, or D. One million?

GEORGE. Why should I answer? It's just going to be wrong anyway.

PERDITA. Guilt –

GEORGE. A! My answer is A.

(The bell dings.)

Of course.

PERDITA. The correct answer was C. There is no such thing as Madrid.

GEORGE. Oh my god.

*(**PERDITA** walks towards **GEORGE** with a car battery and jumper cables. She attaches the cables to the battery and places each clamp in **GEORGE**'s hand, then brings them together to touch.)*

Woah!

*(**GEORGE** throws the cables across the room.)*

What are you doing?!

PERDITA. Trying to kill you.

TWO. Now. Do you, Mr. Henrik, take The Fairest of Them All to be your rawfully wedded wife?

GEORGE. ...no.

TWO. *(To* **PAULYNA.***)* And do you, First Lady Mother Theresa, take Mr. Henrik to be your skillfully breaded husband?

PAULYNA. If the shoe fits.

*(***ONE** *takes a shoe over to* **GEORGE**, *puts it on him, and gives a thumbs up.)*

TWO. *(Bangs gavel.)* I now pronounce you uncle and wife.

GEORGE. I'm an uncle now?

PAULYNA. What are you talking about? You've been an uncle ever since your grandmother was born. Isn't that right, Rhyse?

RHYSE. It certainly isn't left.

PAULYNA. Aren't you sad that I'm married to another man, Rhyse?

GEORGE. That was not a real wedding.

PAULYNA. What's real?

GEORGE. We are not married.

PAULYNA. Of course not. I don't believe in gay marriage.

GEORGE. I'm a man!

PAULYNA. This is awkward.

*(***PAULYNA** *looks down and sees a ring on her finger.)*

Rhyse! You shouldn't have!

RHYSE. I know.

PAULYNA. I love you.

RHYSE. I love you too.

PAULYNA. I'm so glad we're married.

RHYSE. I'm so glad I'm white.

GEORGE. No he doesn't.

PAULYNA. What?

GEORGE. He doesn't love you.

PAULYNA. Of course he does.

GEORGE. I heard him say it. He doesn't love you.

(**PAULYNA** *sticks her hand up the back of* **RHYSE**'s *shirt like he's a puppet. His mouth moves as she speaks.*)

PAULYNA. (*Speaking for* **RHYSE**.) Of course I do.

RHYSE. (*Speaking for himself.*) Love.

PAULYNA. (*Speaking through* **RHYSE**.) I love her so so so so so mu—

RHYSE. (*Speaking for himself.*) Stop.

(**PAULYNA** *stops.*)

PAULYNA. What is it, love of my life and father of my bride?

RHYSE. I don't love you.

(*Beat.*)

PAULYNA. Fear me.

(**RHYSE** *does nothing.*)

(*Beat.*)

Well I always have Henrik. Right, Henrik?

(**GEORGE** *starts to say no, but then stops. He looks at* **PERDITA**.)

(*Beat.*)

GEORGE. Of course. I love you forever.

PAULYNA. Fear.

GEORGE. I fear you forever.

PAULYNA. Let's fearmake.

PERDITA. No he doesn't!

(**PAULYNA** *looks to* **PERDITA**.)

PAULYNA. Perdita. Speaking out of turn…

PERDITA. Don't listen to anything he says. It's all a lie.

GEORGE. I love you!

PERDITA. You're lying!

GEORGE. Not if I say it more!

(GEORGE crosses to PAULYNA.)

Marry me, princess!

(PERDITA slaps GEORGE.)

PERDITA. Why are you doing this?

GEORGE. I –

PAULYNA. Why are you talking to Perdita, Henrik VIII? Do you love her?

GEORGE. No, I don't practice bestiality.

PAULYNA. Well loving Perdita isn't – *(Understands what* **GEORGE** *is implying, smiles.)* The help aren't persons.

GEORGE. Exactly.

PAULYNA. Perdita, take Henrik to a room and give him a million dollars.

(PERDITA pulls out a gun.)

TWO. We have a winner!

(ONE stands up and reads from the dictionary.)

(The following lines by **ONE** *should be read underneath the scene. So* **ONE** *maybe reads the first definition and then the rest of the lines continue while he/she reads them. It would be nice if the definitions somewhat lined up with when the words are spoken in the scene.)*

ONE. Lie. A noun. A statement told with the awareness of its falsehood and the intention of deceiving. "Abe was often known to lie; he rarely tells the truth."

Winner. Noun. One who has won a contest or tends to win them. Or who was said by someone to have done so. "That man is a winner. He won."

Scared. Adjective. To be frightened, worried, or intimidated by something of the similar sort. "I'm really scared. Not really."

Fib. Noun. A statement not always seen to be true, but then again what statement is. "I didn't lie, that was a fib. I didn't shoot you, I just kind of did."

Brave. Adjective. To not be scared, frightened, worried, or intimidated in the face of things of the sort. An honorable state or possibly just ignorant. "He is brave, she is brave, we is brave."

Ignorant. Adjective. To be unaware or to lack knowledge. Bliss. "Ignorant kind of sounds like abhorrent."

Bliss. Noun. See ignorance. "Ignorance is bliss and rhymes with piss."

Want. Verb. To desire, to wish to have, to like, to love, to dance, to prance. "Tell me what you want, what you really really want."

Brother. Noun. A male sibling. Or a male mother. Or a black father. Or an orange sister. "The apple was green. Brother."

Try. Verb. To attempt. Or not to attempt but make it seem as if you did. "Wacka wacka wacka."

Right. Adjective. To be correct or true or Republican or not left. "The answer sounded good, but I don't think it was ride."

Children. Noun. The plural form of child. One's offspring or one who is not of age. A kid. A baby goat. A wish. "A dream is a child your heart makes."

Darling. Noun. Someone who is dear to or loved by another. Like daring with an L in the middle. "Oh my darling, oh my darling, oh my darling, maritime."

Trophy. Noun. An item awarded to someone who has won or we were told had one. Could be a statuette or plaque or wife or fish. "Are people born trophies or do they have trophies thrust up in them?"

Dramatic pause. Noun. A tool used to emphasize the gravity of a dramatic moment. "   ."

Physical conflict. Noun. A conflict that exists in the physical world and does not involve mental struggle. "Todd's mental struggle was a physical conflict."

Believe. To know or think or at least hope that something is real. "Santa Claus is dead."

Santa Claus. Proper noun. Savior of the Christian faith. Born in swaddling clothes and crucified on the cross. Son of the Vegan Mary. "To be or not to be, Santa Claus is the question."

The meaning of life. Abstract noun. Bibbidy bobbidy boo, the cow jumped over the moon, the cat ran away, to roll in the hay, friggity fraggity froo. A poo poo poo, a choo choo choo, a woo woo woo, a goo goo goo. A ga ga ga a ra ra ra ro ma ma ga ga ooo la la watching the Romans. "Life has no meaning."

Just kidding, it does, but I'm not going to tell you what it is. Haha. I'm funny. "Dictionaries are people."

GEORGE. *(To* PERDITA.*)* Put down the gun.

*(*TWO *pulls a box of trophies from under the stand.)*

PERDITA. *(To* GEORGE.*)* Scared?

*(*TWO *hands the box to* THREE *and they walk downstage.)*

GEORGE. *(To* PERDITA.*)* Not in the slightest.

*(*ONE *continues to read from the dictionary.)*

PAULYNA. Wow, Henrik you're brave like my husband.

GEORGE. I'm your husband.

PAULYNA. No, Rhyse is. Right, Rhyse?

*(*RHYSE *pauses.)*

RHYSE. Yes.

GEORGE. What?! What about me?!

PAULYNA. What about you?

GEORGE. What do you want!?

(Beat.)

PAULYNA. To be honestly wanted.

*(*TWO *and* THREE *walk into the audience and begin handing out trophies.)*

*(*ONE *continues reading.)*

PERDITA. *(To* GEORGE.*)* I'm going to kill you.

(GEORGE *and* PERDITA *begin to walk in a circle, as in a shootout.*)

PAULYNA. *(To* RHYSE.*)* This looks fun, brother.

(PAULYNA *and* RHYSE *join the circle and raise their finger guns.*)

(ONE *continues reading.*)

(TWO *hands trophies to audience members as* THREE *follows with the box.*)

TWO. For you, miss. And for you, ma'am. Etc.

GEORGE. *(To* PAULYNA.*)* I'm not your brother. *(to* PERDITA*)* You won't shoot me.

PERDITA. *(To* GEORGE.*)* Try me.

PAULYNA. You're right, Henrik –

GEORGE. *(To* PAULYNA.*)* I'm not Henrik!

RHYSE. *(To* GEORGE.*)* I believe the children are hungry, darling.

GEORGE. I am NOT your darling.

(ONE *continues.*)

(TWO *and* THREE *do so as well.*)

TWO. A trophy for you, sir. You're a winner. And you're a winner.

(GEORGE, PERDITA, PAULYNA, *and* RHYSE *continue their circle.*)

RHYSE. *(To* GEORGE.*)* Sorry, Father. I confused you with the missus.

PAULYNA. *(To* GEORGE.*)* We do look quite alike, don't we, Mum?

PERDITA. *(To* GEORGE.*)* You think I won't shoot?

GEORGE. I know you won't.

PAULYNA. But I will.

(PAULYNA *shoots* RHYSE *with her fake finger gun. He falls to the floor, gasping for air.*)

PAULYNA. My god, are you okay?!

RHYSE. *(Whispering.)* I'm not your god…

PAULYNA. *(Running to* **RHYSE.***)* But you want to be!

TWO. You are a winner, miss. And you. Winner here. Winner there.

*(***RHYSE** *coughs.)*

PAULYNA. Are you dead?

RHYSE. *(Whispering, to* **PAULYNA.***)* The children are hungry.

PAULYNA. Children have to eat?

*(***PERDITA** *shoots* **PAULYNA.** *She falls on top of* **RHYSE,** *lifeless.)*

*(***EVERYONE** *stops for a moment. All is silent.)*

ONE. Dramatic pause. Noun. A tool used to emphasize the gravity of a dramatic moment.

*(***TWO** *continues handing out trophies.* **RHYSE** *crawls out from under* **PAULYNA** *and continues walking in the circle.* **GEORGE** *is speechless.* **PERDITA** *stares down* **GEORGE.** *The children in the background begin to starve.)*

PERDITA. *(To* **GEORGE.***)* Believe me now?

GEORGE. You're a monster.

TWO. Winner. Winner. Winner. Winner.

*(***ONE** *continues.)*

PERDITA. You're dead.

*(***PERDITA** *shoots at* **GEORGE** *but misses and hits* **RHYSE.** *He's dead.* **GEORGE** *runs.* **ONE** *continues.)*

PAULYNA. I'm pregnant!

*(***PAULYNA** *is alive again. She has a baby doll up her dress.)*

TWO. Winner! Winner! Winner! Winner! Everyone's a –

GEORGE. STOOOOOOPPPPPPPP!!!!!!!!!!!!!!!!!!!!!!!!!!!!!!!!!!!

*(***EVERYONE** *stops.* **GEORGE***'s shout wakes* **RHYSE** *up.)*

(GEORGE is standing on a couch USC. He has a gun in his hand.)

PERDITA. How did you get –

GEORGE. Shut up! All of you, shut up!… *(To* **ONE.***)* You! Stop reading definitions. *(To* **TWO.***)* You. Never say the word winner again. *(To* **RHYSE.***)* You. Stop agreeing with everything she *(*PAULYNA*)* says. *(To* **PAULYNA.***)* You… Make sense! *(To* **PERDITA.***)* And you…just. Shut. Up.

(GEORGE loads his gun and points it directly at PERDITA.)

(PERDITA drops her gun.)

(She stares at GEORGE.)

(He gets ready to shoot her.)

PERDITA. Who's the monster now?

(A gunshot. The stage goes dark.)

(After a moment, the lights come back up. The stage is empty except for **GEORGE,** *sleeping in his bed once again. He awakens abruptly. After seeing all is well, he takes a deep breath.)*

GEORGE. A dream… It was a dream.

PAULYNA. What was a dream, sweetie?

*(*PAULYNA *sits up from under the covers. She has a small lamp under her dress, posing as a child.* **GEORGE** *jumps out of the bed.)*

GEORGE. No! No! No! It was a dream! You're not real!

PAULYNA. Of course it was a dream. And so is this.

GEORGE. This isn't real?

PAULYNA. No, it's real.

GEORGE. What?! Why can you never agree with yourself? Why can't you just tell the truth? *(Pause.)* I need to find the truth.

PAULYNA. On the contrary, love. It's not the finding.

(**PAULYNA** *gets out of bed, walks to* **GEORGE,** *and places a hand on his face.*)

It's the making.

(**TWO** *enters.*)

TWO. Paulyna went on to never make sense and have many more children, though no one knows how many.

(**PAULYNA** *crosses and sits down in her spot at the beginning of the show.*)

Rhyse went on to agree with everything she said.

(**RHYSE** *enters and sits down in his beginning spot.*)

The children went on to eat food.

(**ONE** *and* **THREE** *enter and stand next to* **TWO** *in their beginning positions.*)

Perdita went on to talk.

(**PERDITA** *enters and stands next to* **THREE.***)

George went on to never wake up from his dream. Or maybe he did. If it even was a dream. Who can know? The heart maybe? Not you. Not I. No one, I fear.

(**GEORGE** *walks to* **PERDITA***'s laminating station at the beginning of the show and sits. Everyone is ready.*)

ONE, TWO, THREE AND FOUR. And that's the truth.

End of Play

The Christian Soothsayer

by Aaron Robertson

THE CHRISTIAN SOOTHSAYER was presented in a staged reading as part of the Thespian Playworks program at the 2013 Thespian Festival on June 29, 2013. The reading was directed by Mark D. Kaufmann, with dramaturgy by Judy GeBauer, and stage management by Chyanne Fischer. The cast was as follows:

ISAAC..Isaiah Rusk
SCOOT... DeWayne Taylor
ALBERT...George James
ETHEL..Joy Donnelly

Subsequent to the Playworks staged reading, *The Christian Soothsayer* was produced at University Liggett School in Grosse Pointe Woods, Michigan, on February 7, 2014. It was directed by Phillip Moss. The cast was as follows:

ISAAC...Joshua Dickens
SCOOT... Alexander Bowman
ALBERT...Austin Sasser
ETHEL... Jewel Evans

ABOUT THE PLAYWRIGHT

Aaron Robertson, a Detroit native, wrote *The Christian Soothsayer* in response to the work of August Wilson. He currently attends Princeton University, majoring in English and pursuing certificates in creative writing and African-American studies. More than anything else, he loves his two dogs, the cinema, folklore, and thinking about the Midwest. He thanks Dr. Phillip Moss for making the theatre a space for all who would dare to explore it.

CHARACTERS

ISAAC – A con man

SCOOT – Isaac's friend and accomplice

ALBERT – Ethel's loyal husband

ETHEL – A pious woman

All the characters are African American. Albert and Ethel are at least two decades older than Isaac and Scoot.

COSTUME DESIGN

I have referred to Ms. Ellen Keyser's notes on designing costumes for *The Christian Soothsayer* to compile the following list:

Isaac – slightly oversized shirt, gaudy tie, trousers
Scoot – sweater-vest, long-sleeve shirt, pleated slacks
Albert – suit jacket, plain button-up, skinny tie, pleated slacks, hat
Ethel – church-going dress, seasonal hat, purse

GROUND PLAN

There is no order to the scene. A few upturned tables and chairs, and a bar. The stairs to the basement are on the opposite side of the bar.

(Detroit, 1967. The basement of a blind pig. Most of the drinking glasses are smashed; some litter the floor in dark liquid alongside old cigarettes, hats, etc. Many of the tables have been violently overturned, and those that aren't are topped with unlit candles. Most chairs are missing. The place is abandoned save for two African-American men. Both are in their mid-thirties. **ISAAC** *leans against the bar and looks over a bottle of alcohol in his hand. A notepad rests beside his arm.* **SCOOT** *paces, examining invisible details in every disturbed item and scribbling notes on a legal pad.)*

SCOOT. You talk to that cop?

ISAAC. Wilson up there across the street.

SCOOT. I don't know how you got that fool under your thumb.

ISAAC. You know what that man told me? Looked me in the eye and all, he said, "A Negro'll be a Negro, but a moneytalking one blinds me in one eye."

SCOOT. Well then, how he going know when to shoot?

ISAAC. I ain't worried. We going move one of them candles, that's all. Ain't no issue. He asking for about a month's worth of salary. I don't hardly get paid no way. What's a month? But look. When it get bad, if it start looking bad, you going to have to do something, now. You can't just be standing there. You got to make it real.

SCOOT. Yeah, don't worry about what I'm a do. I ain't fresh to this. You got the dice?

ISAAC. *(Continues scrutinizing the alcohol.)* You asking some questions. What I look like?

SCOOT. I got an answer.

ISAAC. Yeah, I got them.

(**SCOOT** *moves around the room, searching, peering at the undersides of tables. Eventually, he finds something.*)

SCOOT. Look at this, here.

ISAAC. Quit digging through them purses.

SCOOT. Why you always think I'm digging through something?

Maybe I just made an observation.

ISAAC. Ain't no need observing them purses.

SCOOT. Let me work.

(**SCOOT** *picks up one of the purses and pushes his hand inside. He comes up with nothing and throws it down.* **ISACC** *puts the drink behind the bar.*)

ISAAC. Ain't no need observing them purses. They already empty.

SCOOT. How you know that?

ISAAC. How you think? (**ISAAC** *reaches into his pocket and pulls out a couple bills, etc.*)

SCOOT. You going to hell, boy.

ISAAC. What was you going do?

SCOOT. Would a replaced them if I could find them. Right in these pockets. Keep them warm for when the Miss comes back.

(*A distant explosion sounds.* **SCOOT** *flinches and a woman yelps from offstage, on the same floor as the journalists.*)

ISAAC. Old Miss probably needs more than a purse.

SCOOT. You still holding that aspirin, Isaac?

(*From stage right, a man and woman appear. They are in their fifties.* **ETHEL**'s *hands cover her face as Albert escorts her to one of the seats. They are well-kempt, although shaken.* **ALBERT** *grabs* **ETHEL**'s *hands and kisses them.*)

ALBERT. (*To* **ISAAC**) You about ready?

(**SCOOT** *prepares his legal pad and pencil while* **ISAAC** *lingers at the bar.*)

Them Negroes getting themselves cut good.

(**ETHEL** *begins praying to herself.* **ISAAC** *grabs his notepad and pulls a chair next to her. He gestures, and* **SCOOT** *pulls another one for* **ALBERT**.)

ETHEL. *(Eyes still shut in prayer.)* Y'all hurry now, please.

ALBERT. We gone be fast, Ethel. Ain't we?

ISAAC. Hope to be. This about as quiet as it is. Least we not up there on Twelfth.

SCOOT. I seen one of them young Negroes stomped near to his life.

ETHEL. And Lord wrap your arms about these children…

ALBERT. These white folks is brutal than the rest.

SCOOT. I ain't mention nothing about them being white. He was being stomped by kids darker than him.

ETHEL. …from the crowns of their head to the soles…

ISAAC. *(Glancing through note pad.)* Mr.…

ALBERT. Albert.

ISAAC. We appreciate you being here with your wife. This ain't going take but a few minutes, willing. This here is Scoot. He—

SCOOT. *(Frowning at* **ISAAC**.) Louis.

ISAAC. …he help me get the articles ready for the paper. He's the editor.

ALBERT. You ain't putting our names there is you? We don't want no attention. We don't want no one at the door.

SCOOT. *(Looks at legal pad.)* Got you down as…Lionel and Grace Richards. *(To* **ISAAC**) You really ain't got aspirin? This headache is going kill me.

ISAAC. I ain't got no aspirin. Mr. Albert, you tell me what you want, anything about the riot. We just writing this down and going to get your word out.

ETHEL. You don't even work for the Press. Who going listen to a Negro that don't work for the Press?

ISAAC. Other Negroes.

ALBERT. *(Looking around.)* Ain't there nothing to drink down here?

ISAAC. People done took everything. This is it.

ALBERT. Too bad. That's too bad. *(Beat.)* We got a place up on Gratiot, near Mack. It's by our church, you know. We was getting ready to leave out for the evening service and this mad Negro start yelling outside. He running up the street with a brick yelling, "Let's get these white mother –!"

ETHEL. Albert!

ALBERT. So, you know, Ethel asking to stay inside. She don't want to go to church no more. She lost the Holy Spirit when that Negro was shouting.

ETHEL. I can't be in the Spirit with that going on.

ALBERT. Now, what you going do when a mad Negro running by your house with a brick? You go outside and beat him until he drop the brick. So I said to Ethel to stay in the house and I'd be back. I grabbed my hammer, went outside, and asked him what he was yelling about. You know what he say?

SCOOT. Hmm?

ALBERT. "Twelfth Street 'bout to burn down!" I ask him what he mean and he talking about the police losing control. Stores being broken into. Then he get ready to throw the brick at my house. So I run at him and start waving the hammer. He don't think I'm going hit him so he start laughing. When I hit his hand he drop the brick and— *(Off* **ETHEL***'s look.)* Say some things that ain't important. They don't need repeating.

ISAAC. *(Writing notes.)* What was you doing, Ms. Ethel?

ALBERT. She shouting at me to get back in the house. I ain't listen, though.

ETHEL. Stubborn. What I'm a do if you get killed?

ALBERT. So I said to Ethel, say, "We going drive down and see what's happening." I wasn't letting her stay in the house no more. I know she ain't want to come, but I wanted to see what this fool was talking about.

(Another explosion. **ETHEL** *resumes praying.)*

Came up on Twelfth and saw them police walking round, looking confused. They was already knowing they couldn't do nothing. Them Negroes had them standing about a hundred yards away. Them streets too. Trash, everywhere. Bunch a trash.

ETHEL. You telling them about what that police did?

ALBERT. So we was going drive back home. Ethel was back there getting worked, she was scared. Shoot. I wanted to get back. Only thing that gets me more scared than white men is vengeful Negroes. They don't know no colors. If you scared in your eyes they see that and you better move. Ain't no black or white.

(A long pause. **ETHEL** *looks at* **ALBERT**, *the journalists, then to her husband again.)*

ETHEL. Ain't you going tell them about that police?

*(***ALBERT*** *does not acknowledge the question.)*

SCOOT. What they do?

ETHEL. *(Beat.)* This one police stopped us. He start asking if we was about to join the riot. I say, "I ain't messing with you." Then he ask to see what's in the car. He say he got to search it for "dangerous possessions." What we look like with dangerous possessions? He tell Albert to step out...

ALBERT. They don't need no more.

ISAAC. We just trying to tell the truth, Mr. Albert.

ETHEL. ...He tell Albert to step out the car. We ain't trust that police for a minute before he start looking around. Then he go and grab our Bibles and toss them down. *(Pause.)* You hear me?

ISAAC. I hear you.

ETHEL. That police worked me up. I got back to the car and picked them Bibles up and the police grabbed my arm like this, about this hard. Albert try getting him off and the police smack him with a baton—

ALBERT. They don't need no more, Ethel.

(Beat. **ISAAC** *reaches into his pocket and pulls his hand out in a fist, holding something small.* **SCOOT** *notices and looks at* **ISAAC.***)*

ISAAC. There's something I ain't getting about all that.

ALBERT. What you mean?

ISAAC. *(Pointing upstairs.)* The streets. All that fire.

ETHEL. Just people being mean.

ISAAC. Ain't that, Ms. Ethel. I been walking these streets for a second. Been in and up around this place. I done talked to everybody. Jews, Negroes, Japanese. And ain't but one thing that's going comfort them when this is over.

ALBERT. What you saying?

ISAAC. Well, people going blame it on something, ain't they? The whites'll judge the Negroes, Negroes bound to judge the whites.

ALBERT. That's the way of things.

ISAAC. Naw. Once they get done blaming each other, they only got God left to blame.

ETHEL. That ain't new. People been blaming God since birth.

ISAAC. *(Rolling the items in his fist.)* Ain't you been too, Ms. Ethel?

*(***ETHEL** *does not acknowledge this accusation.)*

ALBERT. Show your respect.

ISAAC. All I'm suggesting is that ain't no one free of that. I mean, when the sun fall, we ain't blaming ourselves. We just asking who going pick it up.

ETHEL. You done?

*(***ISAAC** *empties the contents of his hands onto a nearby table. Three dice.)*

SCOOT. What he meaning to say is that things is wild. That's the nature of all this. Ain't that it, Isaac? That's why we out here. I got two girls waiting on me back home, but you know what I tell them? I says y'all sleep because your father going be back one way, the other. They eight and six. They don't know nothing about all this. That ain't my job to tell them. My job is to come out here, places like these, remember everything I saw, and tell my girls about something different. If they want the truth, they can know when I'm fresh and dead.

ETHEL. Ain't that so.

ISAAC. Lemme ask you this. I ain't got to write this down. You in my confidence. Can I ask?

ALBERT. Go ahead.

ISAAC. How much faith you got?

ETHEL. Oh, here he go.

ISAAC. I mean, we all here is Christian, ain't that so? I know Scoot is.

SCOOT. Hell, I'm Catholic.

ISAAC. You about as Catholic as my foot.

SCOOT. *(Genuflecting to mock-kiss* **ISAAC**'s *feet.)* I knew when I seen them these was some holy feet!

ALBERT. Yessir.

*(***ISAAC*** looks to ***ETHEL***.)*

ETHEL. Boy, you ain't hear me talk? Christian before I knew what it was.

ISAAC. Well, I'm asking, how much faith you got? We all in agreement here. We don't need no secrets.

ALBERT. I don't see what you getting at. This ain't for the paper?

ISAAC. This not for the paper.

ALBERT. I been in the faith for, what, going on twenty years.

(He smiles at **ETHEL***, who returns it in equal measure.)*

It was my life anew then. Ain't stopped moving forward. I got enough faith to keep me standing, all right.

ISAAC. *(Pointing to the dice.)* This where I keep my faith.

ETHEL. *(Looking straight at the dice.)* On the table?

> *(ISAAC grabs the dice and rolls them around in his hand while ETHEL and ALBERT watch cautiously. ISAAC tosses one of the dice so that it lands on the table. He rolls the remaining dice in his hand, throws one, rolls the final die, and throws that. SCOOT looks at each of the dice.)*

SCOOT. *(Murmuring under his breath.)* Four…one…

ISAAC. *(Looking at the die nearest him.)* That's three.

SCOOT. *(Staring at the dice and rubbing his head.)* Times that by three. So, fifteen… Shoot.

ALBERT. What's the matter with you?

SCOOT. It ain't nothing. My head just bothering.

ISAAC. You two is some good faithfuls, I can see that.

ALBERT. *(Pointing at the dice.)* What you doing there?

ISAAC. This? Ain't nothing but a little pastime. I mean, it's faith, sure. It's hope and life and all those things. But it's just a pastime too.

ETHEL. It ain't nothing but gambling to me.

ISAAC. May so.

SCOOT. You ever seen how the dice work? It ain't a labor. Look, here. *(SCOOT picks up all three dice and rolls them like Isaac was doing.)* What you do is shake them round for a minute. Then you throw them one at a time, like this. *(SCOOT demonstrates.)* You can just drop them too. Then you count the numbers on each. Them two that's further away, you add them numbers. This one here by me you going multiply by—

ISAAC. It don't matter none to them. There's some special about it if you do it right, though.

ALBERT. *(Skeptical.)* And what's that?

ISAAC. You ain't going believe it if you hear it. Scoot here learned it a while back. He wasn't no believer either. What I'm saying is, because we people of faith, there's some things God make special to us. Some things can't nobody else understand.

ETHEL. Yes. A Christian who pray is all the wiser than someone that don't believe.

ISAAC. You not wrong, Ms. Ethel. But I'm talking about God saying things through us using, well, using other things. I ain't meaning no stuff of demons or none of that. You believe God gives us gifts, yeah?

ALBERT. Man, what you getting at? Say what you getting at.

ISAAC. I just don't want to give you no reason to doubt. I'm saying the numbers on these dice say things. Messages. Like prayers being answered. You believe He answers prayers.

ALBERT. Well, now that's—Isaac I'm only telling the truth as I know it. You can't doubt a man from the Word.

ETHEL. You up here with these dice. What Word is you reading that talk about some dice?

SCOOT. I mean, all respect, Ms. Ethel. We in changing times. When the world change, some parts of the Word change. Not them basic things like love or adultery. But how God…talk to us.

ALBERT. (*Standing, grabbing* ETHEL'*s hands.*) We gone. You ain't talking nothing good.

ISAAC. (*As* ALBERT *and* ETHEL *approach the exit.*) That story you wasn't wanting Ms. Ethel to finish.

(ALBERT *stops and turns.* ETHEL *continues facing the exit, listening.*)

What was that story?

ALBERT. That ain't nothing you got to worry about. What paper you working for again?

SCOOT. Give him a chance, Mr. Albert. Listen, here.

ISAAC. I know what you ain't wanna finish. I know about that police and what he did to Ms. Ethel after you got knocked down.

(ETHEL *freezes.* ALBERT *begins walking toward* ISAAC *and* SCOOT *moves in the way.*)

How I'm going know this if it weren't God?

ALBERT. You don't know nothing.

(**ETHEL** *says something too quietly to be heard. To* **ETHEL**.)

What you saying?

ETHEL. *(Turning to the others.)* I want to hear what he got to say.

ALBERT. This boy fooling you, Ethel. He don't know nothing.

ISAAC. 'Bout how that officer started feeling Ms. Ethel.

(**ETHEL** *gasps.* **ALBERT** *glares at* **ISAAC**.)

I ain't fooling you. You want me to say where that officer was feeling Ms. Ethel? I ain't in no mood to talk about it, really. *(Pause.)* How he done touched Ms. Ethel's...

(**ALBERT** *pushes* **SCOOT** *aside and lifts* **ISAAC** *by the neck.* **ISAAC** *holds his hands out and looks to* **ETHEL**, *who watches in horror. As soon as he regains stability,* **SCOOT** *rushes to separate the two.)*

ALBERT. You a low nigger, boy.

ISAAC. Now call me that again.

ETHEL. How do he...?

SCOOT. It's them dice, Ms. Ethel. Them dice.

ALBERT. I ought to smack you down.

ETHEL. Albert...

ALBERT. You hush, Ethel.

ISAAC. I ain't meaning to hurt you. God just been putting you on my mind. He wanting me to help you. And you calling me an animal? Now, Mr. Albert. I look like one of them folk outside? We got to use better language than that.

ALBERT. You ain't no journalist. Ain't no help I see.

SCOOT. We are writers, true to the word. We ain't working for a big paper, though. They don't want none of us working at the big papers. They scared we going tell the truth.

ISAAC. You going hear what I got to say? You welcome to leave.

(**ALBERT** *does not make for the exit. He waits.*)

This good, that you're staying. It's going help. I know where that police is.

ETHEL. ...and guide Your hand of mercy as we cross these straits...

ISAAC. He out here tonight. Them streets is lit with them store fires, so he plain as day.

ALBERT. What the hell I look like trusting you? You not listening to no God.

ISAAC. The policeman was touching Ms. Ethel round two minutes before some more Negros start coming to you. Tell me I'm lying. Tell me I'm lying, Ms. Ethel.

ALBERT. Don't say not a word to her.

SCOOT. This only the truth, Mr. Albert. That's all.

ISAAC. You can go about denying it. But you'd be better trusting what I got to say.

(**SCOOT** *reassumes his seat, keeping his eyes on* **ALBERT**, *who motions for* **ETHEL** *to stand beside him. His eyes are intent upon* **ISAAC**.)

ALBERT. Now you got to understand something. They's some things a man ain't expected to tolerate. He's probably best to take some words that sting insomuch as it makes his skin thick. But ain't nothing in no Bible in the world that say he got to listen to one disrespecting his wife. I ain't read that passage just yet. You going call it what you want.

ISAAC. I was doubting it too when I knew I first could do it. Just fooling. Then I roll some numbers and start knowing something was different. Now, I don't be knowing everything. They's some things God see fit to keep to Himself. He got his secrets too.

ETHEL. You just a lie.

SCOOT. He true as life. A year back I'd a been like, this one of them hoax Negroes. I was like you. But Isaac. He blessed. He a late apostle if they ever was one. Fresh John the Baptist. Brand new Philip of Galilee.

ISAAC. Them police ain't going know where you are if you listen, here. I know where to find that one who messed with Ms. Ethel.

SCOOT. He do. I seen him round here.

ALBERT. *(Beat.)* I believe you a tricky Negro. I don't know what to believe. Them dice ain't telling you nothing. But I don't know what you been doing to know about that policeman.

ISAAC. That ain't nothing but the Goodness above. So you want to know? I'll tell you if you listening.

ALBERT. We gone, Ethel. *(To* **ISAAC.***)* You unhealthy.

SCOOT. Mr. Albert?

ALBERT. What you saying?

SCOOT. Now, I'm a honest man. Will you let me be honest? I been married for about since I can remember. Nineteen, twenty years old. If they's anything I learned, it's that my lady know how to treat me right. I ain't just talking about what she do to sustain me. Irene—she know what I feel. All I can try and do to show how I appreciate her is promise to live like a man. That mean if someone goes and touch Irene…well. A man can't just watch from above his feet. You know what I'm about.

ALBERT. If you think I'm a fool enough to reply to that, you wrong. If you honestly think.

SCOOT. I ain't pestering. I just don't know no man that won't get back they woman's honor.

ALBERT. We ain't talking about nobody's honor.

SCOOT. 'Cause all I know, if one man that ain't got my blood place they hands on Irene. If they so much as sniff her hair without my knowing. Well. Let's leave it at that. I ain't calling you a lesser man. I'm just telling what I would do.

ALBERT. You hear me asking what you would do?

ISAAC. *(Gathering the dice in his hand.)* Scoot, you stop now. Mr. Albert don't need no pushing.

ETHEL. Oh, why you messing with a man's pride? He ain't do no harm towards you. He just being the best he can. This is a good man. Now I know y'all can see that. He ain't no bother.

ISAAC. No, he ain't no bother.

ETHEL. Albert been working all his life for me. He up at that car factory near every day. And I'm thankful for that. I don't need him to be looking for no more trouble.

ISAAC. *(Rolls one die.)* That policeman you looking for. He out there by the Chinese hand laundry. Next to the party store. You know the one? Across from the barbeque place?

ALBERT. What?

ISAAC. I seen him coming here. He got this big group of Negroes around him. Them other police trying to help, but we got them beat for now. It's going change, sure enough. You looking to get at him, now'd be the time.

(A bright spark and the lights go out, hissing and cracking. ALBERT moves to hold ETHEL while SCOOT stands and checks the lights. ISAAC continues rolling the dice in his hand. Now, the only illumination comes from the moonlight spilling through the basement windows.)

ETHEL. What's that?

(So as not to burn himself, SCOOT wraps his hand in his shirt to untwist the bulb from its socket. He twists it back in, but the light does not come on. He moves to a light switch in the room and flicks it with no result.)

ISAAC. That's the power.

(Moving to the candles on one of the tables.)

Ain't no one got a light?

SCOOT. *(Patting his pockets.)* Aw, hell. I ain't got one. Wait… hold up. Here it is.

*(**SCOOT** pulls a lighter and tosses it to **ISAAC**, who lights the candles. He moves around the room and lights the candles that are on the other tables and in small nooks. Finally, he places three candles in a row against the window looking out at the street.)*

ISAAC. That's going do for now.

SCOOT. How the power going go out?

ETHEL. I'm about ready to leave, Albert.

ISAAC. *(Tosses the second die.)* I ain't gone say not to, but it's probably them rioters outside the place. I don't mean they right outside. But I bet they near enough to see anyone leaving.

ALBERT. You still messing with them dice. You a fool. This place be getting torn down and you just going be sitting here with your hands up talking about dice.

ISAAC. They ain't lying. I knew these lights was going go out.

ETHEL. He frightening me, Albert.

ISAAC. I know something else too. You better avoid them windows. *(Pointing to the window lined by candles.)* One of them rifles going bust it up. Boom! Going bust the glass all over this floor.

*(**SCOOT** moves to **ISAAC**'s side. **ALBERT** shuffles away from the potential trajectory of the shrapnel. **ETHEL** remains still.)*

ETHEL. You sound a fool. *(To **ALBERT**.)* And what you doing moving away like he talking some truth?

ALBERT. I ain't bothering you. I don't know nothing about this fool.

ETHEL. You know he ain't right in the mind. Don't you?

ALBERT. I don't know nothing about him.

ETHEL. Like I do. Let's get home.

ALBERT. *(Looking to the candle-lined window.)* We just may. It look mighty hot out there, though. Ain't no telling how we can move from here.

ETHEL. *(Moving to the exit.)* Same way we came in, cut through that back alley. *(Beat. To* **ALBERT.** *)* You going come?

ALBERT. *(To* **SCOOT.** *)* You best to turn your eyes from me. *(To* **ETHEL.** *)* Don't be giving me no looks like that, Ethel.

(Neither **ETHEL** *nor* **ALBERT** *moves.* **ALBERT** *'s eyes dart between the three faces staring at his own.)*

What you eyeing me like you mighty?

ETHEL. Come on, Honey. Ain't nothing out there but me and you.

ALBERT. It's hot out there.

ETHEL. You not—you ain't believing none of this, is you?

ALBERT. I ain't believing no fool. I don't know what to believe.

ETHEL. Look at me. You ain't got to be scared of nothing. But it's all right if you is. You believe me now, it's all right.

ALBERT. Ain't nobody scared. I'm looking out for you.

ETHEL. I know you are. You looking out for me.

ALBERT. That's right. You talking to me like I'm some child. Like I don't know what I'm saying.

ETHEL. No, I ain't doing that.

ALBERT. I'm out here protecting you.

ETHEL. It ain't me you got to be mad at, Honey. These boys deceiving you.

ALBERT. They ain't running out there to get killed. We just going wait for a minute. Let the air get cleaned up a bit.

ISAAC. That police ain't staying out there long.

ETHEL. Albert, look at me. We just going walk out there. I'm going grab your hand and you going hold mine and we just moving to the car. Ain't but what, but twenty feet.

(**ALBERT** *stares out the window.* **ETHEL** *smiles.*)

Oh, Lord. Look at you.

(**ETHEL** *starts walking towards the window.* **SCOOT** *looks to* **ISAAC,** *but Isaac only extends his hand for him to stay put.*)

This ain't nothing to be afraid of. We going bring one of these candles to the car.

ALBERT. Get from the window.

ETHEL. Albert…

ALBERT. (*Watching* **ISAAC,** *who continues rolling the dice.*) I said get from that window.

ETHEL. It ain't hurting you.

(**ETHEL** *picks up one of the candles and* **ISAAC** *leaps to grab her, yanking her away. Barely two seconds later, a loud crack and the glass shatters completely, spilling on the floor where* **ETHEL** *once stood. She screams and Scoot jumps.*)

SCOOT. Shit!

(**ISAAC** *moves to console* **ETHEL.**)

ETHEL. Get that devil from me! Oh, Lord. Oh, Lord.

ISAAC. You see, I ain't talking no cheap stuff. I ain't meaning to hurt y'all. I'm trying to help.

ETHEL. Don't touch me!

SCOOT. It's warming up out there, Isaac. I see the lights. They getting brighter. What we goin' do if they come in here?

ISAAC. They ain't got no reason to. Everything already gone.

SCOOT. They don't know that.

ISAAC. You trust me, Scoot.

SCOOT. I do. I trust you. But—

ISAAC. (*Moving to* **SCOOT.**) What's the matter with you, boy?

SCOOT. It ain't nothing but my head. I'll take something for it when I get home.

ALBERT. Ethel. Ethel, baby, you doin' fine? You doin' all right, Ethel?

ETHEL. *(Badly shaken.)* Yes, Albert.

ISAAC. You fine, Ms. Ethel?

ALBERT. Don't let her name drop from your tongue again. You hear me?

ISAAC. You know this ain't nothing but wrath. This just God wanting you to do what he ask. I mean, it's up to you to listen. That ain't nothing I can do for you. Neither can Scoot. I ain't your enemy. Look, here. *(Extending his open palms for* **ALBERT** *to see.)* There ain't no spot for me to be scrubbing.

ALBERT. Where them dice?

ISAAC. You saying what?

ALBERT. Them…them dice.

ISAAC. Now can't but some people use—

ALBERT. I ask you what can some people do?

(Reluctantly, **ISAAC** *gathers the two dice he threw onto the table surface and hands them to* **ALBERT**. *The third one rests in the pile of glass.* **ALBERT** *walks over to it, moving the glass with his feet and—when that proves ineffective—digging with his hands. He picks up the last die.* **ETHEL** *looks to* **ALBERT**, *and all the fear of what he is about to do is confirmed by the slight aversion of his eyes. To* **ETHEL**.*)*

You ain't got to look at me that way. I ain't doing no fool's game now. I'm showing you how he just a lie. *(Rolling the dice in his hand.)* How he don't know a damn thing about nothing. About no God, no policeman. Them streets is hot out there tonight, Ethel. They burning and ain't you or me about to walk out on them. This fool don't know nothing. *(Tosses one of the dice. Reads the number to himself.)* You know, Ethel, I ain't mean to let that policeman go on like that. I ain't mean for him to trifle with your sense of being a woman. I just…sometimes man get scared is all. *(Rolling the dice.)* I done my best for you. You know that. I try to put some meat on your fork, sweat through the day knowing you goin' wipe it off my face and smile like you ain't never seen me a day in your life. You know what smile I'm talking about? *(Tosses another die. Reads the number to himself.)* Your face just glowing and that's why I go out every day. I take some stuff from anybody. I go and I see people broken down 'cause they ain't got no money or nobody to go home to. I seen people near die cause they ain't got no one like you to smile at them. But I got that hop in the back of my foot because I know I do.

ETHEL. You stand up, now.

ALBERT. *(Rolling the last die.)* I ain't mean to let that policeman do that to you. What a man I am. You know how strong I am? I'm crawling on the floor, my face all in the dirt. And while that policeman grinning, I just stay there and don't get up. Ain't that hard to see that I could stand. I could stand well and beat that policeman to the ditch. But I'm just laying there. And I don't move.

(**ALBERT** *tosses the final die. He can no longer look at* **ETHEL,** *nor anyone in the room. A light coming from outside seems to grow in intensity with each passing moment.* **SCOOT** *peers into the brightness and grabs his head.)*

Where you say that policeman was?

ISAAC. What?

ALBERT. That policeman.

ETHEL. *(To* **ISAAC.)** You best to save your soul now. You be good to tell something honest.

ISAAC. He out there by that Chinese hand laundry.

ETHEL. You going tell him that lie?

ISAAC. You know the one? You know what I mean?

ETHEL. *(To* ALBERT.*)* He ain't telling no truth. You can see that. You ain't got to look at him and you can see he ain't nothing but one lie.

ISAAC. *(Pointing to the shattered window.)* I'm a lie?

ETHEL. You don't got to believe him. Ain't you listening to me? Ain't you hearing me talk no more?

ALBERT. I don't know.

ETHEL. You don't...

ALBERT. *(Gazing at the stairway leading upstairs.)* I don't know what to believe.

ISAAC. It's your Christian duty, that's all.

ALBERT. *(Weakly.)* What you know about being Christian?

(ALBERT *approaches* ETHEL, *avoiding her gaze. He grabs her hand and brings it to his lips. He edges toward the stairs, not looking back.)*

ETHEL. You know what you about to do. Don't you go outside. The streets ain't safe. If you a man, you going show that to me now. A man value his life. He respect that people need that man in they lives.

ALBERT. *(Looking to the exit, not at* ETHEL.*)* Them streets is open to me. *(Beat.)* I'm going give that policeman a word for you, Ethel. You ain't got to come. It's just going be me and him.

ETHEL. You a fool if you step outside them doors.

ALBERT. Where else I got to go?

(ALBERT *begins his slow exodus up the stairs and* ETHEL *does not move after him. Instead, she draws her coat collar around her neck, watching as her husband disappears.)*

ETHEL. Why you doing this?

ISAAC. What you saying?

ETHEL. You heard well enough.

ISAAC. This is nothing but—

ETHEL. Just stop that. Stop that mentioning God. Stop all that talk about things you don't know. I know your type of spirit. It ain't a fiber worth saving. Why you going let a man walk out into that mess?

(**ISAAC** *walks behind the bar. He brings out the bottle of alcohol he had previously stored and finds two unbroken glasses. He sits and opens it.*)

ISAAC. That's just it, Ms. Ethel. I ain't doing a thing. I'm here, looking at you. Mr. Albert, though. He walking into the fire on his own accord.

ETHEL. Your mind is wrong.

ISAAC. No, I'm a true believer. You and me, we can look at something as solid as a rock and see it differently. You think I'm messing with God, but I ain't. I know where it ain't good to meddle. You see Him and you thinking about some invisible hand splitting the skies and people murmuring about how much that hand done for them. Okay. Well, I got a different take. You seen how it is. How people do. You think all the Negroes was born to sing in unison? That chaos is the white man's doing? Now, Ms. Ethel. You a wise woman. Go on outside and see for yourself. They not thinking about no hand in the sky or singing no hymns. They just want to break into them stores and grab what they can get while they can get it.

SCOOT. Isaac, boy, the noise outside. That noise. Ain't you done? Them rioters moving back up…

ISAAC. We all right, man.

SCOOT. Come on, Isaac.

ETHEL. I ain't never seen a soul more spiteful. I can only pray for you.

ISAAC. Try for me, Ms. Ethel. Your god ain't my god. My god is outside there, quickstepping in the fire. I always been a man of this city and I had me some good brothers and some fine sisters there to hold me on up. But here come a little rousing and rumbling and what do we do? We forget the gospels we was weaned on, lose every scripture to the dust. The great plight of the Negro is that he wallows and wallows for alms. And just as fast, he be the one to cut his own man down. You and me in another world, Ms. Ethel, could a been dukes. But we settle for the brandy instead.

ETHEL. What you talking about another world? Ain't none but this. You and me ain't nothing alike but for the skin.

ISAAC. Now that's the truth. We part of a proud race, Ms. Ethel. That pride puffs us up, bolsters that God you love. But in another world, just think of what lives we'd lead. Dark-skinned dukes and duchesses.

ETHEL. And you send a honest man up there? That's not what I'm getting. Why send a God honest man in that mess?

ISAAC. (Pouring one glass.) I ain't nothing but a little curious. Mr. Albert seen everything I did here. Now, I ain't push him to go outside. I just showed him that it's all right to do things on your own, is all. It's better that people see that sometimes, you understand? For people to feel like they control they own lives. He could a stayed right here. Could a choked me to death if he had wanted it bad enough.

ETHEL. That wasn't my husband walked out there. You playing them mind games with him and you don't even understand what you doing. He went out there because of you. Your heart ain't in the right place.

ISAAC. (Placing his hand across his chest.) It's just right here. You looking for someone to push for your troubles then you look to yourself. He out there for your honor, ain't he? Like I say, I just been here with y'all. My heart innocent as ivory. But if that's all the Negro man is meant to be, fools like Mr. Albert, then Lord let me not be one of them. Say it with me now. Amen.

ETHEL. I been blessed not to have met many people like you. I seen my share. I forgot how ugly they could be. (ETHEL *moves to the stairway and looks up. She pauses before beginning the climb to the top.*) You tell me this. I already see through you. You ain't got to lie. How you know anything about that…that policeman?

ISAAC. *(Pouring the other glass.)* Go on outside, Ms. Ethel.

*(**ETHEL** decides against a response. She trudges up the stairs and is gone. **ISAAC** drinks from his glass and starts gathering the writing material. As he passes **SCOOT**, he glances to the stairwell.)*

Don't let me forget to save some drink for Wilson. Ain't no easy man to get on a job. Let me see another Negro go up to a white cop like I done. He get beat, I guarantee. You been listening to all that, right? I don't know what I'm a call that.

(He continues pacing around the bar, picking up discarded items from the floor and re-organizing chairs. He comes to an item he hadn't seen before and picks it up.)

Hey. Look here, Scoot. You missing a purse.

SCOOT. I'm… Isaac?

ISAAC. What you saying, Scoot?

SCOOT. Isaac?

ISAAC. What you want?

SCOOT. I swear I ain't been here before in my life.

ISAAC. What?

SCOOT. This blind pig. I ain't set a foot in this place.

ISAAC. What you talking?

SCOOT. Come on, Isaac. You heard. Louis Bernard ain't never set a foot in this place!

*(The light outside grows more intense. **SCOOT** stares into it and turns to **ISAAC** as if in a daze. When another explosion occurs—louder than it had been previously— **SCOOT** falls to the glass-covered floor. A seizure. The way his body convulses is reminiscent of some fantastic exorcism. **ISAAC** hurries to his side, unable to assist.)*

ISAAC. Scoot. Get up, now. Scoot, we got to go. You can hear me, can't you? Them rioters… All right, you lay there then. You keep playing and you lay there. But you got to get back home, and I can't be the one to tell your wife... Scoot?

(There is no response. **ISAAC** *stands and backs away from the body, staring down at it. The light from outside continues to grow. Upstairs, yelling and crashing.)*

You quit playing, Scoot. We got to find Wilson. He'll pull us out.

*(***ISAAC*** *resigns to the floor.)*

That's all right, Scoot.

(The door to the basement opens, and the illumination of fire spills through into the darkness.)

Say it with me now...

End of Play

The Crib

by Steve Rathje

THE CRIB was presented in a staged reading as part of the Thespian Playworks program at the 2013 Thespian Festival on June 29, 2013. The reading was directed by Carolyn Greer, with dramaturgy by Nicholas C. Pappas and stage management by Dorann Matson. The cast was as follows:

HEATHER . . . . Grae Greer
MOTHER. . . . . .Katie Irwin
MATTHEW/MAN . . . . Ryan Maltz
WOMAN . . . . .Julia Sismour

ABOUT THE PLAYWRIGHT

Steve Rathje, a native of Portland, Oregon, wrote *The Crib* during his junior year at Lake Oswego High School. He'll soon be a freshman at Stanford University, where he plans to continue playwriting; his other interests include acting, psychology, and communications. Steve has written several one-act plays and has co-written two musicals with his brother. His work has been recognized by YoungArts, Young Playwrights Inc., Blank Theatre's Young Playwrights Competition, and the Scholastic Art and Writing Awards. His plays have been produced at Portland's Fertile Ground Festival of New Works, Westview High School, Lake Oswego High School, and the Oregon State Thespian Conference. He would like to thank everyone on the Playworks team, especially Nick Pappas, Julie York Coppens, and Carolyn Greer, for making Playworks an unforgettable experience and teaching him so much about the craft of playwriting—and his parents and his brother, for their continued support of everything he does.

CHARACTERS

HEATHER – 20s
MOTHER – 40s or 50s
MATTHEW – 30s
MAN – 30s
WOMAN – 20s or 30s

Note: **MATTHEW** and **MAN** are played by the same actor. Also, the crib and the bed may be conveyed by the same set piece. The set should be sparse and surrealistic.

(**MOTHER.** *enters. She is holding a camera. She lifts her camera and begins filming an unseen character. She speaks:*)

MOTHER. Heather. I have to make this video. They want to see if you're responsive. They want you to wiggle your fingers or something. Or else they're going to kill you. So do me a favor and smile for the camera like you did when you were a girl, okay? I know it's hardly a time for smiling. They all think you're dead. We'll show them.

(**MOTHER** *exits.* **HEATHER** *steps off of a train platform. She carries a suitcase with her. She is lost. She takes a few steps forward and takes in her surroundings. She drops the suitcase. A man sneaks behind her and steals the suitcase.*)

HEATHER. Hello?

(*She wanders the stage, looking for someone.*)

Is anyone here?

(*She reaches for her suitcase and discovers that it is not there. She tries to get back on the train, but it has already left. A* **WOMAN** *walks up from behind her.* **HEATHER** *turns around.*)

You scared me. Did you take–?

WOMAN. No.

HEATHER. Do you know when the next train will come by?

WOMAN. You must be here for the procedure.

HEATHER. Yes, I am.

(**WOMAN** *takes out a clipboard.*)

WOMAN. Sign here.

(*She does.*)

And here.

(She does.)

And here.

(She does.)

HEATHER. What exactly am I agreeing to?

*(***WOMAN*** puts away the clipboard.)*

WOMAN. You can read it later. Wait here.

HEATHER. Will it hurt?

WOMAN. Yes.

HEATHER. Is it reversible?

WOMAN. Are you sure you want to go through with this?

HEATHER. I'm sure.

WOMAN. Wait here.

HEATHER. Do you have a waiting room or anything? With a couple magazines, some soft chairs, a fish tank?

WOMAN. No.

*(***WOMAN*** exits. ***HEATHER*** sits on the ground. The man who took her suitcase walks behind her. ***HEATHER*** doesn't notice. ***MOTHER*** enters.)*

MOTHER. Heather! What are you doing here?

HEATHER. Waiting.

MOTHER. For what?

HEATHER. A procedure.

MOTHER. What kind of procedure?

HEATHER. A small thing.

MOTHER. Do you have any paperwork I can read?

HEATHER. The nurse has it.

MOTHER. I want to know about this.

HEATHER. I know what I'm doing, Mom.

MOTHER. Heather…

HEATHER. You make me nervous.

MOTHER. You've always been nervous. When you were little you used to hide behind my leg whenever we were around people. You've never really changed.

HEATHER. Yes I have.

MOTHER. I'm just trying to calm you down. You shouldn't do something that makes you this upset. I won't let you.

HEATHER. Mom!

MOTHER. We're going to stay here and wait for the next train home.

HEATHER. I don't think the train's coming.

MOTHER. It has to. Trains don't just disappear. I don't care how long it takes. I'm going to wait here with you until we get to go home again.

(**MAN** enters. He is carrying **HEATHER**'s suitcase, but she doesn't seem to notice.)

MAN. Heather? We are ready for the procedure.

MOTHER. She's not going.

MAN. And who are you?

MOTHER. I'm her mother.

MAN. Heather is twenty years old. She gets to make this decision herself.

MOTHER. Do I at least get to know what you're doing to her?

MAN. I believe Heather requested we not disclose that information.

MOTHER. (To **HEATHER.**) I want you to tell me exactly what –

MAN. We are very qualified and can assure you that your child will remain –

MOTHER. I won't let you!

(**MOTHER** grabs **HEATHER**.)

HEATHER. Mom!

MAN. Nurse!

(WOMAN *enters and separates* HEATHER *from* MOTHER. MAN *and* HEATHER *exit.*)

WOMAN. Don't worry. I have to do that all the time. With the kind of procedures we do...

MOTHER. What do you do?

WOMAN. I don't really know myself. But, I overheard Heather telling the doctor that she didn't ever want to have children...

MOTHER. Is she pregnant?

WOMAN. No, but she doesn't ever want to be, so I'm guessing –

(*We hear* HEATHER *offstage.*)

HEATHER. *(OFF)* No, I change my mind, I change my mind, I don't wanna do this anymore I change my mind –

MAN. *(OFF)* We're finished, Heather, I can't...

MOTHER. Heather? Heather?

(WOMAN *tries to comfort* MOTHER. MOTHER *runs after* HEATHER. *A shift.* MATTHEW *and* HEATHER *are both in bed.* HEATHER *gets up and begins getting dressed.*)

MATTHEW. Come back to bed.

HEATHER. I'm afraid the bed's going to suck me in like a vortex and put me in a deep sleep that I can't come out of.

MATTHEW. She's only out of town this weekend. Do you really want to spend our time together this way?

HEATHER. We have to talk, Matthew. Because. Let me put it this way: I've never slept with a man who has tried to kill me before and maybe if we talked about it I wouldn't feel so –

MATTHEW. It was a complete misunderstanding.

HEATHER. I know, but my mom knew –

MATTHEW. Why do you always bring up your mom?

HEATHER. Because she was right. And I know you two aren't exactly –

MATTHEW. She hates me.

HEATHER. But that's understandable. And it's like. I owe her for being alive today. And I know everyone can say that about their own mothers, but she brought me into the world twice. And maybe if we all sat down. Had dinner together –

MATTHEW. You want us to all have dinner?

HEATHER. We have to talk about this.

MATTHEW. I have a new mother-in-law.

HEATHER. I hate you.

MATTHEW. We were having such a good weekend. And I think it's too soon to really –

HEATHER. Too soon? It's been years!

MATTHEW. I know but –

HEATHER. We'll be dead by the time you think it's okay to talk about it.

(HEATHER *gets up.*)

I'm sorry. You're right. Let's enjoy the weekend.

(*She looks out the window.*)

Such a nice view. Oh my God, look at your deck!

MATTHEW. Yeah, Lisa and I decided a deck was mandatory when we were looking for a home.

HEATHER. And you have a swing set! Remember when we were in high school and I had one like that in my backyard?

MATTHEW. And we'd sit in it for hours and stare at the sky.

HEATHER. We were such nerds back then.

MATTHEW. Thank God we found each other.

HEATHER. My mom liked you then.

MATTHEW. Until we got married.

HEATHER. Yeah, she went crazy over that.

(*Beat.*)

How are they?

MATTHEW. What?

HEATHER. The kids?

MATTHEW. Oh. They're cute, you know? They're twins. Sometimes I can't tell them apart. I never thought of myself as a dad. But, Lisa really wanted them. They just started talking. One of the little guys looked me in the eye and said "Dada." And you see them do things. Crinkle their noses or something like that. And I'm like. That's me. I do that. And it's like. Where does that come from?

HEATHER. Stop talking.

MATTHEW. Not talking might be best. Come back to bed?

(A shift. We are now in a hospital. The bed becomes a hospital bed. **MOTHER** *enters.)*

It's been twelve years. We have to move on with our lives!

MOTHER. What if she was your child?

MATTHEW. She was my wife.

MOTHER. You have a new one. A replacement. Mother and daughter…that is forever.

MATTHEW. I can't believe you're –

MOTHER. You're afraid. You're afraid of what would happen if she did wake up. You're afraid that Lisa would know she's your second choice.

MATTHEW. This is about Heather. What's left of her.

MOTHER. Would you do this to your own child?

MATTHEW. This is about Heather!

MOTHER. I thought you said we have to move on with our lives.

(A shift. The bedroom, again. **MATTHEW** *comes back and sits on the bed.)*

MATTHEW. I thought you were suffering.

(Beat.)

How could I have known you had a life inside your head?

HEATHER. My mother knew.

MATTHEW. Neither of us did. We were both just trying to do what was best for you, whatever we thought that was. How could I have known I was wrong? I can't go back to before, Heather.

HEATHER. Then why are we doing this? To remind me of the great life I had before?

MATTHEW. I couldn't give you up completely.

HEATHER. Then don't!

MATTHEW. I love Lisa.

(*Beat.*)

I waited for you, Heather. I waited so long. I couldn't do it anymore. I thought I was going to spend my whole life waiting. I tried.

HEATHER. Try to help me out when I'm actually conscious.

(*A shift.* MOTHER *enters.*)

MOTHER. Heather. Please. I know you're there. Wake up. Remember when I read *Sleeping Beauty* to you when you were a girl? She woke up. But, Matt's not really your prince. He's quite the opposite. You don't need a prince. Because if you don't wake up this week you'll be gone forever. Please. Or if you can't do that. Just wiggle your fingers. But only when the camera's on, okay?

(*The hospital bed becomes a lavender crib.* HEATHER *gets up and looks into it.*)

I wanted to grow old and sit in a rocking chair watching my grandchild play.

HEATHER. Me too.

MOTHER. I wanted to die knowing a part of me would not die.

HEATHER. Me too.

MOTHER. Watch you hold your newborn – like I was watching myself holding you.

HEATHER. Me too.

MOTHER. Why did you have to wait?

(Beat.)

They want you to wiggle your fingers or something. I tell them: how does the ability to wiggle fingers decide whether or not someone should live or die?

HEATHER. I don't know how to wiggle my fingers anymore.

MOTHER. Try. You don't have much time left.

(Beat.)

Why did you leave it empty?

HEATHER. My time was cut short.

MOTHER. I know about the procedure. He told me.

(Beat.)

HEATHER. I didn't want to be a stay-at-home mother. Or send my children to dirty day-care centers.

MOTHER. You didn't have to…

HEATHER. Or drive them to little league or ballet classes and socialize with other parents.

MOTHER. That's silly…

HEATHER. I didn't want to become you!

MOTHER. What?

HEATHER. I know that's what you wanted to see. You wanted to look at yourself in third person.

MOTHER. No, honey…

HEATHER. Maybe I didn't want to lead the life you planned out for me.

MOTHER. It is not selfish of me to expect grandchildren – just something in return for all of the love I've given you.

HEATHER. That was the past, Mom! This is my life now. This is all I've known. You. Me. My thoughts.

(Referring to the crib)

That. So why talk about that life? That life is over.

MOTHER. Because that life isn't over for me.

HEATHER. It is for me, and you don't need to keep dragging me back into it.

(A shift. The bedroom. **MOTHER** *exits, and* **MATTHEW** *enters.)*

I thought we were so certain.

MATTHEW. What?

HEATHER. The decision to never have children.

MATTHEW. We were.

HEATHER. The procedure was final. I can't change my mind, like you did.

MATTHEW. We were twenty years old, then.

HEATHER. You sound like my mom.

MATTHEW. A lot changed when you were gone.

HEATHER. Without the kids you would have come back to me.

MATTHEW. I'm not staying because of the kids.

(Beat.)

I love Lisa.

HEATHER. You love me.

MATTHEW. Loved. That was the past.

HEATHER. If I had kids I'd have friends. Talk to the other moms while dropping my kid off at day-care. Little league. Ballet.

(Beat.)

God. That is exactly what I didn't want to become. What's happened to me?

(A shift. The hospital. **WOMAN** *and* **MOTHER** *enter.)*

WOMAN. The judge looked at the videos. He ruled they were inadequate, and they're going to go ahead with it.

MOTHER. Did you not tell him how she smiled when I read to her…

WOMAN. I told him what I saw. And what I saw was a twitch.

MOTHER. A twitch? Since when does a twitch look like that? A Mother knows a daughter's smile. She smiled when I read her *Sleeping Beauty.* It was her favorite story.

WOMAN. You're making yourself see things that aren't there. He's made the decision. I can't do anything about it.

(Handing her paperwork.)

Here are the documents. You should say your final good-byes.

(WOMAN gives her paperwork and exits. MOTHER rips up the papers.)

MOTHER. Heather. Bad news. We only have a few days left. Remember how you smiled when I read to you? They thought it was a twitch. But, twitches don't look like that. You always used to fall asleep when I read to you. We'd never finish a book together. I didn't mind though. But, now I do. So please. Wake up. So we can finish the story.

(MAN enters. The hospital bed becomes a crib, again.)

HEATHER. Who is that man?

MOTHER. Ignore him.

(HEATHER walks over to this man. MOTHER talks to the WOMAN, who has re-entered.)

MOTHER. You can't do this! She is living, just not functioning physically...

HEATHER. Who are you?

(The man shrugs.)

Why are you here?

(The man shrugs, again.)

MOTHER. *(To WOMAN.)* You aren't her mother...!

HEATHER. What do you do?

(The man shrugs, again.)

MOTHER. Did you not see how she smiled when –

HEATHER. *(Referring to the crib.)* Can you take this away for me?

MOTHER. You don't know that there is a whole world inside of her head...

(The man takes the crib and drags it offstage.)

HEATHER. I wonder why I didn't think of that earlier.

MOTHER. She doesn't remember how to wiggle her fingers.

HEATHER. It feels so spacious in here now...

MOTHER. You have found nothing because you are looking in all the wrong places!

HEATHER. I've been living in my mind, alone with my thoughts and my mother for twelve years...

HEATHER. And just today you showed up out of the blue and took that useless crib away. Thank you.	MOTHER. ...Where was I in this decision?! Wait, I haven't... just let me... What are you doing?

MOTHER. Don't touch that. STOP THIS RIGHT NOW!!!

(Silence.)

HEATHER. It's so quiet in here. It's like no quiet I've ever known.

MOTHER. Her pulse is slowing down.

MAN. Come with me.

HEATHER. What?

MAN. Take my hand.

MOTHER. You didn't have to...!

HEATHER. Where are you taking me?

MAN. Away.

MOTHER. *(To HEATHER.)* Come back here...

HEATHER. But, I'm perfectly content here.

MAN. This isn't what you wanted to have happen.

MOTHER. Stay away from that man!

HEATHER. But, what about...

MOTHER. Heather!

MAN. Don't tell me you're staying because of her.

MOTHER. Stay with me!

HEATHER. She has no one else. I've left no one else…

MAN. The crib's gone, now.

(**MAN** *holds out his hand.* **HEATHER** *takes it. They begin walking offstage, hand in hand.* **MOTHER** *enters.*)

MOTHER. Heather! Honey! Don't go with that man. Please, Heather. Mother knows best. Come to mother. Look at mother. LOOK AT ME!!!

(**MAN** *turns* **HEATHER** *to* **MOTHER** *to let her say goodbye.*)

Mama. I'm Mama. You're Heather. Mama. Heather. You look at me like a stranger. Like the world is so new. So friendly. With that little tuft of hair. Those tiny toes. Your smile. One day, you're going to grow up to be like Mama. And you'll have a baby of your own. And she'll look just like you.

(**HEATHER**'s *eyes begin to shut.*)

Oh, baby's getting sleepy. Too much excitement – looking at this big world for the first time. Here, let me put you in your crib…

(*She looks around.*)

Oh my God! Who took the crib?!

(**HEATHER** *and* **MAN** *walk off, holding hands.* **WOMAN** *takes* **MOTHER**'s *hand and tries to pull her offstage.*)

You took it! Give it back – you're not taking that or my daughter!

(*To* **HEATHER**.)

Stay with me. You are my only child! It means everything. To not be left behind.

(**MAN** *pulls* **HEATHER** *offstage.*)

You left nothing behind.

(A shift. **MOTHER** *exits. The crib rolls back onstage.* **HEATHER** *enters, looks into the crib, and smiles.)*

HEATHER. Look at you. That little tuft of hair. Those tiny toes. Your smile. Matthew was right. You look just like him.

(She picks up the baby and rocks him back and forth.)

Mama. I'm Mama.

(The baby wakes up. He begins to cry.)

Don't cry. Mama's got you. Shh. Wow, you're certainly a loud little guy. That must be the Lisa in you. Shh. Don't cry. I was kidding about Lisa.

(The baby calms down.)

There you are. Take a little nap in my arms. I'll keep you safe and warm, little sleeping beauty.

*(***MATTHEW*** enters.)*

MATTHEW. What are you doing?

HEATHER. Oh. I'm. Nothing.

MATTHEW. Why are you…

HEATHER. I just wanted to see what it was like. To pretend.

(Pause.)

I think he likes me.

MATTHEW. You're very good with him. Gentle.

HEATHER. He looks just like you. That's exactly what you look like when you sleep.

MATTHEW. You watch me sleep?

HEATHER. I'm sure you've watched me sleep much more.

MATTHEW. Right. I'm sorry.

HEATHER. Matthew. I'm over it.

MATTHEW. He never sleeps this well when Lisa's around.

HEATHER. Really?

*(***HEATHER*** holds the baby close to her. She looks at ***MATTHEW***. She dreams. Then she abruptly sets the baby down.)*

I think I should go.

MATTHEW. He's not going to like that. He's already grown attached to you. He won't want to be separated.

(The baby cries again.)

See.

HEATHER. I can't. I'm not his mother.

MATTHEW. He doesn't like his mother as well as you.

HEATHER. Trust me. He'll learn to. Eventually.

*(A shift. **MOTHER** enters.)*

MOTHER. Heather. Good news. They saw something. Just as they pulled the feeding tube. And it wasn't a twitch this time. You shot up. And moved. Spoke. It was incomprehensible. But you looked like you were calling for help. They're giving you a second chance. We have hope, Heather. I'll have my daughter back soon enough.

*(**MOTHER** exits. A shift.)*

MATTHEW. I thought this is what you always wanted.

HEATHER. It was.

MATTHEW. Then why not? You have to admit. That was pretty magical, what just happened.

HEATHER. You love her.

MATTHEW. I love you.

HEATHER. Loved. That was the past.

(She grabs her suitcase and begins to leave.)

MATTHEW. We could be really happy together. Like we were this weekend.

HEATHER. I wasn't happy this weekend, Matt.

*(**HEATHER** leaves. **MATTHEW** sits for a moment, alone. A shift. We are now in the train station. **MOTHER** and **HEATHER** enter. **HEATHER** is carrying her suitcase.)*

MOTHER. You're so close Heather. Like I said. Trains don't just disappear. You'll be able to wiggle your fingers, again.

HEATHER. Mom. I know that I left nothing behind. But, it's been exhausting. To hear all the voices around me, talking about me, thinking I'm gone, thinking I can't hear them. To know that life is passing by rapidly and not to be able to do anything. I've played it all out in my head. When I wake up I won't have anything to come back to.

MOTHER. What are you saying? You'll have me. The train will be here soon enough.

HEATHER. Mom. I'm waiting for a different train.

MOTHER. But, we're so close Heather!

HEATHER. This is my choice. Not yours, not Matthew's. The only choice I've ever made, myself.

(She picks up her suitcase.)

MOTHER. I've only been trying to do what's best for you. No one tells you how to raise a child. I was sort of on my own.

(MOTHER *and* **HEATHER** *hug.* **HEATHER** *gives* **MOTHER** *a kiss on the cheek.)*

HEATHER. I think you did very well.

(We hear the sound of a train coming.)

It's here.

(HEATHER *exits, gripping her suitcase firmly.)*

End of Play

Houdini Will Die

by Sage Voorhees

HOUDINI WILL DIE was presented in a staged reading as part of the Thespian Playworks program at the 2013 Thespian Festival on June 29, 2013. The reading was directed by Joe Norton, with dramaturgy by Stephen Gregg and stage management by Eve Mendoza. The cast was as follows:

DAVID ....Brandon Crichfield
HELEN... Michelle A. Rodriguez
TERRY ....Ethan Vander-Broek

Prior to its development and staging at the Thespian Festival, *Houdini Will Die* was produced as part of Albuquerque Academy's Thespian Manifesto in December, 2012. The cast was as follows:

DAVID .... William Held
HELEN.. Tara Partow
TERRY ....Renata Hartman

ABOUT THE PLAYWRIGHT

Sage Voorhees, native to fair New Mexico, wrote the first drafts of *Houdini Will Die* in the summer of her junior year at Albuquerque Academy. She is currently an undergraduate at Stanford University, where presumably she will major in something. She is eternally indebted to her family, friends, Richard Hogle, the wonderful *Dramatics* staff, and the Ethiopian goat herder who discovered coffee.

CHARACTERS

DAVID – A scientist, late 40s to mid 50s, trying to develop a drug that will enhance memory. He himself has poor memory retention.

HELEN – The loving wife of David, late 40s to mid 50s. Always "stops to smell the roses" and wishes that her husband would do the same.

TERRY – (Male) An overeager intern, mid 20s, works with David on his research.

SETTING

DAVID is sitting on the couch in the center of the living room. The room is tastefully decorated, but messy: books, coats and notebooks are scattered about. The room is filled with various flower arrangements. In the center of the room are a few wire cages and a large rat maze.

TIME

The present.

(**DAVID** *is sitting on the couch, head in hands. A doorbell rings.* **TERRY** *enters, answers the door.*)

TERRY. Thank you. Yes, I'll be sure to give it to him. Yes, thank you. *(Pause.)* Okay I will. (**TERRY** *closes door, now with a bouquet in his hands)*

Some more flowers for you. (**DAVID** *is not listening, but rather stands up and walks to the rat maze.)* Where do you want me to put these? *(Pause.)* I'll put them on the shelf for now. You can put them in a vase when we get back from the service. They won't wilt too quickly, more preservatives in these flowers than anything else. Isn't that right… David?

DAVID. What?

TERRY. More preservatives in the flowers than anything else.

DAVID. Oh, right.

TERRY. At least their preservatives smell better than ours.

DAVID. Hmmm?

TERRY. The formaldehyde, well it isn't exactly perfume.

DAVID. No, certainly not.

TERRY. I guess I'm getting used to it.

DAVID. Oh. Sure.

TERRY. Do you remember how long it took you to get used to it?

DAVID. Uh. No.

TERRY. Oh, right.

DAVID. It couldn't have been more than a month though.

TERRY. Oh, that's good news.

DAVID. Certainly. Only a week or so now.

TERRY. Well actually, I'll have been working in the lab three months as of Monday.

DAVID. Oh? It's been that long.

TERRY. Yeah, started on the 7th.

DAVID. Oh right. Of course.

TERRY. Came on two batches ago. Working on this project the time has just flown by.

DAVID. Yes. Flown by. *(Pause.)* Flown by—what's that poem, December is... December is here before it's...?

TERRY. I don't think I know it.

DAVID. No, I'm sure you do. You must, it's a famous one. December is here before it's—

TERRY. Who's it by?

DAVID. I can't—

TERRY. Oh, of course.

   (Beat)

   Are you ready?

DAVID. Terry, could I...

TERRY. Yes?

DAVID. Could I have a few seconds, just us?

TERRY. Just...oh. Well, we have to go soon, how much—

DAVID. I forgot my papers.

TERRY. What?

DAVID. My papers. My briefcase, I wanted to bring them with me.

TERRY. But you won't have time to look at them while we are at the service.

DAVID. We're so close.

TERRY. Well, I know that but—

DAVID. Please. I know it's senseless, but please I just want to have them with me. I won't look at them, I just need them with me.

TERRY. Okay. *(Pause,* DAVID *looks at* TERRY *expectantly.)* Do you want me to get them?

DAVID. They are in the study.

   *(*TERRY *exits.)*

Thank you.

*(*TERRY *exits.* DAVID, *after wandering about a bit, kneels at the rat cage, eventually picks up his clipboard of notes and, after writing a few things, picks up an audio recorder. He clicks it to begin, and releases a rat into the maze. As he speaks into the recording device, he sounds monotonous, scientific.)*

RAT 67D, the seventh rat in variable group 5; injected with 2ml HL78. The rat is hesitant to start and seems to have slower movements than those in the control group. At 7 seconds the rat moves to the first test, DP7. A test to measure the retention capability for a learned course. *(Break from monotone.)* No. come on! Don't go backwards, progress through the—ah. That's right, there we go. *(Back to monotone.)* Minor error one… The rat chooses the left gate, the same route which held food three weeks ago when the trial began, the fifth rat in Group 5 to choose the correct course. *(Break monotone in excitement.)* Which shows that this dose has substantial effect on the memory capacity of the— *(Back to monotone.)* The rat has traveled to the second testing point. Takes the third opening, again, the route taught at the beginning of the study. The rat is moving on. Running through. Which shows that… which shows that. *(Breaks from monotone, turns off audio recorder)* What? What does that show? What does that prove? Nothing. It proves nothing. What if it is just luck. Just coincidences. What if that is all any of this is. Oh look! He's past another checkpoint, and chosen the green. What if he just likes green?

*(*HELEN *enters,* DAVID *bends down and picks up the rat.)*

HELEN. David! David put that poor rat down!

DAVID. Helen! Sorry, I was just trying to—

*(*DAVID *fumbles trying to put the rat back into the cage.)*

HELEN. Are you crazy? He's going to be here soon.

DAVID. Who is?

HELEN. Terry. David, are you feeling alright?

DAVID. Terry?

HELEN. Terry, your intern? He is going to be here in a few minutes. The service starts at six.

DAVID. Yeah of course, I was just teasing. I was waiting for you to get out of the shower.

HELEN. Waiting?

DAVID. You take forever.

HELEN. David.

DAVID. Sorry.

HELEN. I thought you said you wouldn't bring them home.

DAVID. What?

HELEN. You promised me you wouldn't bring work home this weekend.

DAVID. Helen, I thought I—

HELEN. You told me that we would go on a hike tomorrow. After the funeral.

DAVID. I'm sorry, it's just that –

HELEN. You promised me, David. You said we would go up to the old trail and have a picnic, like we used to—

DAVID. I know.

HELEN. And this weekend? Of all weekends there will be people everywhere. Where will they sit—

DAVID. What do you want me to do? Take them back to the lab now?

HELEN. We were going to have a feast. Take a basket up to the route nine trailhead. Have a nice little hike, then lunch, like we used to.

DAVID. I'm sorry, I forgot. *(Beat.)* I didn't have a choice. I had to bring them home. We're so close, it's different for this formula. But next weekend I promise. No, I swear. I swear we'll go on that picnic and it'll be the best picnic, the best picnic you could dream of. French nobility will drool at our splendor.

HELEN. David.

DAVID. What? I promise Helen, I promise.

HELEN. It's always next weekend.

(**TERRY** *enters, hesitates at the door.*)

DAVID. It'll be different this time. I wont forget. Trust me.

(*Pause.*)

TERRY. I couldn't find it.

DAVID. Find what?

TERRY. The briefcase.

DAVID. It wasn't on the counter?

TERRY. I thought you said it was in the study.

DAVID. Did I?

TERRY. Yes. You— (*Deep breath.*) Is it on the counter?

DAVID. I'm sorry.

TERRY. I'll go look again.

DAVID. Thank you.

(**TERRY** *exits.*)

HELEN. So he is here.

DAVID. Yes. Sorry I didn't mention it... Why are you laughing?

HELEN. It's just funny. I don't know. Just thinking, he's here and I didn't know it.

DAVID. And that's funny?

HELEN. I don't know, it's hard to explain really. It just is.

DAVID. Oh.

HELEN. Your rat escaped again.

DAVID. What?

HELEN. Your rat.

DAVID. Shit.

(**DAVID** *scrambles to retrieve the rat. He fails to do so.*)

HELEN. Isn't that the same one that escaped last week, the white one with black ears?

DAVID. It's not.

HELEN. Are you sure?

DAVID. It can't be. I reinforced that cage last week.

HELEN. No, no I'm sure it was the same one—

DAVID. No, that rat was eighty something, 86A maybe. *(DAVID consults his notes.)* And this one is... Oh. Good memory.

HELEN. You should name him Houdini

DAVID. *(Attempting to catch Houdini.)* I never name them. Dammit, I almost had him.

HELEN. You don't even name them?

DAVID. Of course not. *(Makes a dramatic leap for Houdini, misses and bumps his head.)* Dammit that hurt. Of course not, what would that do, imagine if we had to fill our data with all sorts of names. What would we do, alphabetize? It would be ridiculous.

HELEN. Oh yes, that would be *completely* ridiculous.

DAVID. Could you be quiet, this is difficult.

HELEN. You can't distinguish between them. You know that's probably why they escape.

DAVID. They're just rats.

HELEN. So?

DAVID. Well what do you expect us to do with them, name them, brush them individually, put them in retirement homes, train them for little kid parties. *(He catches the rat.)* Aha, got her, uh, him.

HELEN. Call him Houdini.

DAVID. Houdini?

HELEN. It's a good name, lots of luck in the name.

DAVID. Luck?

HELEN. Houdini was born poor. I read about him the other day in that book Martin gave us. He was born in Budapest, came over to America when he was four and grew up in some town in Wisconsin... Appleton maybe? Anyway, his father was the first rabbi there.

Can you imagine that? The son of a poor immigrant and he ended up the highest-paid star in Vaudeville.

(**TERRY** *enters.*)

TERRY. David, I can't seem to—

DAVID. Terry! Oh I'm sorry I almost forgot you were here for a moment.

TERRY. Sorry to startle you.

DAVID. No, no. It's okay. *(Pause.)* I remember where it is.

TERRY. The briefcase?

DAVID. Yes.

TERRY. David, we really need to get going.

DAVID. The second you left the room I remembered. It's in my car.

TERRY. Your car?

DAVID. Could you look for me?

TERRY. If I find it can we go?

DAVID. Yes. Of course. I just…

TERRY. Yes?

(beat)

DAVID. The car is unlocked.

TERRY. Okay.

(**TERRY** *exits,* **DAVID** *follows him to the door and locks the door behind him.*)

DAVID. It was all fake, you know. Houdini. Just tricks.

HELEN. But he had a lot of luck. Talent too. And he knew how to handle things without fear, perilous situations and such. You've got to give him that.

(Beat.)

DAVID. Listen, they're rodents. They don't need dignity. They just need food. That's what makes them perfect.

HELEN. What are you doing all of this for, David?

DAVID. What?

HELEN. You heard me. *(Pause.)* Why are you doing this—

DAVID. Do you remember the night I got the grant?

HELEN. Yes.

DAVID. You know what's funny.

HELEN. What's funny, David.

DAVID. I thought that was the hard part. That night, I thought the hardest was over. I had gotten the money. You remember how much I got?

HELEN. Of course I do.

DAVID. That's funny, because I don't. We've spent it all already. Whatever it was wasn't enough. Isn't that funny. Wasn't enough.

HELEN. It will pay off soon.

DAVID. It might not. I think that we're onto something, but who knows. Who knows anything? *(Laughs.)* I thought it would be easy. No, not easy, but doable. Feasible, a drug to boost memory, we knew what we were looking for, we had leads, years of other people's research. And what, we've added research.

HELEN. Necessary research.

DAVID. Oh yes, *necessary* research.

HELEN. Then what are you doing this for.

DAVID. Because it… well, I…

HELEN. See, there is your problem.

DAVID. Because I'm not Houdini, Helen! I can't just pop out of a straightjacket and call it my life's work.
(Pause.) Imagine it Helen. If we never forgot. Or, if *I* never forgot. Not just the facts and names. But never forgot the faces. Never forgot the little things, the details.

HELEN. So you spend your whole life staring at rats, noticing every whisker and tick? *(Pause.)* If you are trying to preserve memories, David? Then why not make some too.

DAVID. Helen, that's not fair.

HELEN. I'm leaving, David.

DAVID. What?

HELEN. I'm leaving. You'll be free, David, all of the time. You can bring work home whenever you want, leave the house in a mess, drink milk out of the carton, save the world with your experiments, whatever you want.

DAVID. Helen, Helen please!

HELEN. It's okay. I understand. I get it. You have to work because you don't want to live without "making advances," "moving forward." Your whole life is one damned selfless effort, one more... what did you say at Janet's brunch?... "one more light in the face of vapidity"? Yes, that was it. David, I... Well I...

(Pause, shift in mood, gently chiding.)

It's a mess in here. A week and already it looks like a pigsty.

DAVID. It's not that bad.

HELEN. Sure. And food? Have you been eating?

DAVID. I've been eating enough.

HELEN. Has my office called you yet? They might be a bit upset that I've left them so suddenly.

DAVID. I love you.

HELEN. Oh and there are some things at the drycleaners that need to be picked up.

DAVID. I love you.

HELEN. What are you doing?

DAVID. Helen, I love you. Don't go.

HELEN. David. It's too late. I don't have a choice.

DAVID. Of course, of course you don't have a choice. None of us do. *(**DAVID** looks at the maze, after a pause he begins tentatively miming a wall.)*

HELEN. What are you doing. David! What are you doing?

DAVID. They're clever. You know that, they are clever. Much more so than I am. See that maze, poorly constructed at best. But not this one, you can't even tell where the walls are, but they're here.

We're no better than they are, these rats. They run through their life, they scamper through our experiments and somehow we are made to feel superior, but we're not, Helen. Not you, not me, not the best Nobel Prize-winning scientists in the world.

HELEN. *(Not listening.)*

Make sure that you visit your dad.

DAVID. But you could try, try to stay. We both could try harder. Maybe they made a mistake in the construction, some loophole.

HELEN. *(Ignoring* **DAVID.** *)*

And the flowers. Please water them. The roses out front especially. And enjoy watering them too. Don't think of it as a chore because it's not, not if you do it really slowly.

DAVID. But it all can change, Helen.

HELEN. Change?

DAVID. We can just swoop down and change everything they know. And all the while they run to get the bait. Because that's what they do. They run to get the bait. They run to feed themselves. They run to sleep. It's that simple.

HELEN. *(Laughing.)* Simple?

DAVID. That's the problem. It *is* simple. Yet we try to inject some meaning into it because we are so caught up in the idea of our own magnificent importance. And sure, some are magnificent. But the unimportant ones try just as hard, they never stop.

HELEN. David, David calm down. Please.

DAVID. I can't.

HELEN. You've always been one for the dramatic.

DAVID. I'm serious, Helen.

(Long pause.)

HELEN. Maybe Houdini is named after a man who faked his audiences. And maybe he will never be part of a scientific breakthrough. *(Beat.)* But David? Houdini lives. It's... well, it is simple. But why is that bad?

DAVID. I'll be better. I'll be a better person, try harder to be neat. Just don't go. I'll trim the fruit trees too and make sure your garden has all the flowers I can find and—

HELEN. No you won't.

DAVID. I can try.

(**TERRY** *enters, tries to open the door. The handle twists, but* **DAVID** *has locked him out.*)

HELEN. He's back.

DAVID. Already?

HELEN. I have to go.

DAVID. Can't you just wait a second? Just a few minutes more?

HELEN. David.

DAVID. Please.

HELEN. Alright, a few seconds.

(Beat.)

Do you have anything to say?

DAVID. What if I forget?

HELEN. Forget what?

DAVID. Anything. Your favorite food, the way you smell when you come out of a shower, what if I forget everything?

HELEN. There is nothing I can do—

DAVID. Please, just one more thing. Tell me one more thing, something I can remember.

(Pause.)

HELEN. Do you know the first thing you said to me, David?

DAVID. It was so long ago.

HELEN. Are you sure? Come on. Try, David.

DAVID. I can't do this, Helen, all I remember is what I've written down. You are the one who knows, not me.

HELEN. Just try, David, where were we?

DAVID. At a bus stop. I remember that. We were... well, we must have been waiting for the bus.

HELEN. Good. And then?

DAVID. And then we sat together on the bus.

HELEN. Because there were no other seats.

DAVID. Because you were beautiful.

DAVID. Oh. *(Pause.)* It was a poem. Dr. Seuss. Wasn't it?

HELEN. Yes, you looked out the window and when you turned back you said, without any explanation, without introduction, without anything—

DAVID. "How did it get so late so soon? It's night before its afternoon...

HELEN. ...December is here before it's June. My goodness how the time has flewn...

UNISON. How did it get so late so soon?"

(Beat.)

HELEN. Say goodbye to Houdini for me.

(She exits. TERRY knocks forcefully on the door.)

TERRY. David? David what's going on?

DAVID. Just a minute, Terry.

TERRY. I found the papers. Are you ready?

DAVID. Just a second.

(DAVID answers the door, lets TERRY in.)

TERRY. David... What's going on? Who were you talking to?

DAVID. What? I was just... I was just.

TERRY. Come on, let's get that lab coat off.

DAVID. I was just...

TERRY. It's okay. I have directions to the funeral parlor but we'll need to hurry, Helen's eulogy starts at six. *(pause)* David?

(**DAVID** *takes the briefcase from* **TERRY**, *then goes to the cage where he put Houdini and releases the rat and sets down the briefcase.*)

Goodbye, Helen.

(**DAVID** *walks off stage,* **TERRY** *remains onstage until the blackout.*)

End of Play

www.ingramcontent.com/pod-product-compliance
Lightning Source LLC
Chambersburg PA
CBHW070632120726
47909CB00004B/1404